The Galty Prize

An Irish Story

by

Jean Tolle

SUMMARY: A nineteenth-century Irish girl hopes to bring back her family's land by winning The Galty Prize steeplechase, its trophy and gold. Along the way she must confront hard truths and make a fateful choice.

CATEGORIES:

Young Adult and Adult   Ireland -19th Century
  Historical Fiction   -Horses and Horse Racing
Coming of Age   -Immigration from
                                                 -Home Rule

Published by

JED Books   Cover Art by Jeffrey Tolle
P.O. Box 3091   Book Design by DunbarDesign
Barrington, IL 60010
JeanTolleBooks.com

Printed in the United States of America by LightningSource and distributed by Ingram. Additional copies of The Galty Prize can be purchased from the publisher or through bookstores nationwide.

ISBN 0-9773590-0-4   ISBN-13 978-0-9773590-0-4
Library of Congress Control Number: 2005909426

Author's Note: Maggie Shannon, her family, friends and enemies live only in imagination. I have attempted to make the setting against which they move as faithful to the history of the time and place as I could. The needs of the story caused me to move the Fairy Woods of Blarney Castle north to County Tipperary.

ABOUT THIS BOOK

Those who know me well will not be surprised that I began writing about Maggie, Joe, Brendan and the horse, Pegasus, when I was about Maggie's age. It isn't that I write particularly slowly, but I revise a lot and add things when I learn something new about Ireland or my characters. Sometimes I've thought the book was finished and then found that it wasn't nearly complete. Also, in between beginning and finishing, I wrote several other books, raised my children, taught school—also tried to learn to fly, play tennis and golf, things I was never very good at.

One thing that I know is true about writing a book is that, for this writer at least, it can't be done without love, support and lots of editorial help. I am truly grateful for my wonderful husband Ed and my children, Jeff and Anne, who, along with their spouses, Judy and Ron have cheered me on. Special thanks to Jeff for the beautiful cover art of this book, and Anne for help with publicity and news releases.

Jasmine Candlish directed me to texts that educated me about Irish history and she pretty much walked with me into the dismal swamp of early drafts. In those days, Linda Girard, Marsha Portnoy and Sandy Berris enriched the writing—some of their suggestions jump out at me with every re-reading. The late Mary Craig was an astute mentor.

Anna Murray, the late Colin Murray, and Mary and Thomas O'Reilly, helped with Irish words and phrases; they even gave me the name Bran for Maggie's dog. Bran means crow in Gaelic. Readers will find that Bran, the dog, is white; they may take it that the name then is ironic, like naming a kitten "Tiger."

iii

Members of the Barrington Writers Workshop encouraged, questioned, and gave me answers; I hope they will forgive me for not writing all their names on this page, but they have my undying gratitude. Laura Rennert, who was my agent for a time, helped a lot with one of the final rewrites. Thank you, Janice and Rob Dunbar of DunbarDesign for making a beautiful book. Thank you all. I love you.

Jean Tolle
July 6, 2005
Barrington, Illinois

TABLE OF CONTENTS

Chapter 1
The High King's Horse 1

Chapter 2
The Fairy Woods 10

Chapter 3
Under the Rowan Tree 18

Chapter 4
A Leprechaun's Penny 25

Chapter 5
The Ruined Field 29

Chapter 6
The Gypsy Mare 34

Chapter 7
A Favor of the Hoof 41

Chapter 8
"A Powerful Cure in This Box" 47

Chapter 9
"Don't Let the Fever Take Her Down" 51

Chapter 10
"She'll be a Flyer" 58

Chapter 11
A Special Gift 63

Chapter 12
Saddle and Ride 72

Chapter 13
"Maggie Shannon on the Tinker's Horse!" 77

Chapter 14
A Heavy Bag of Gold 87

Chapter 15
Soldiers Far From Home 92

Chapter 16
On the Road to Cahir 98

Chapter 17
Poets and Patriots 104

Chapter 18
An Unwelcome Reminder .113

Chapter 19
Victory Flags 120

Chapter 20
Grandfather 124

Chapter 21
A Desperate Wager 130

Chapter 22
High Hopes 134

Chapter 23
Party for a Sixteenth Birthday 137

Chapter 24
Unwelcome Guests 143

Chapter 25
A Different Race 146

Chapter 26
Bullets and Treason 157

Chapter 27
New Beginnings 168

Glossary 177

⊰ CHAPTER 1 ⊱

THE HIGH KING'S HORSE

I n County Tipperary, Ireland, March is a time of
daffodils and morning dew upon the grass. When I
shut my eyes, I see the blooms meander like golden
rivulets through our pasture and I feel the damp grass
beneath my feet.

In memory, I return to the daffodils. It is 1868, my
thirteenth year, and I am unaware of all that is to happen,
unaware of triumph and defeat about to perch like twin
birds on my two shoulders.

When I am sixteen I will have felt both, the elation
and the sorrow—love and danger besides.

I, Maggie Shannon.

*****

1

When I woke in the sleeping loft, that morning three years ago, my brother Joe was not in his bed across from mine. I guessed that he had risen early to tend the cows. Our dog, Bran, must have gone out with him. And so, for that moment, our small family was only the two of us, Grandfather and me.

Grandfather sat warming himself before the hearth. I had served his morning stirabout porridge and a mug of tea and settled down to enjoy my own. Grandfather wore the broody look that I feared might stamp his face forever.

I wanted to give Grandfather something to hope for, more than a potato at noon and another for supper. I wanted to bring back the old days when he owned the acres on which we lived, the days when fine steeplechase horses grazed our rich grass—before those pastures were put to rye and oats for the benefit of others.

"Tell me about Brian Boru, Grandfather," I asked.

In the familiar story of the High King of Ireland, maybe I would get the courage and inspiration I needed to bring back Grandfather's happiness, some of his joy. Maybe High King Boru could give me that.

I scooted my creepie stool closer to Grandfather's chair, to catch his every word. At thirteen, my legs had grown too long for me to sit comfortably on the creepie, but I loved its position at Grandfather's knee. I loved knowing how his own hands had carved its seat and set three stubby legs to the base. Before it became mine, my brother Joe had used it and, before that, our father, when he was a boy.

"It was in the very old times, Maggie, that the giant, Fomor, came out of our own Galty Mountains to challenge Boru for the crown of Ireland," Grandfather said.

2

He told how three times King Boru's gallant Ossian outraced the wind to defeat Fomor's horse—according to Grandfather, a horse "with iron hooves and a neck round and strong as an oak tree."

"And fire-breathing, Grandfather." I wanted nothing left out.

"Ah, yes, Fomor's horse was fire-breathing, but even so, it could not conquer the horse of Boru. Twice the two horses battled each other for a lead in the final race. First, one nosed ahead and then the other. Then, just before the finish, Ossian surged into the lead once more. Fomor's horse, unable to match the effort, fell to its knees, its heart bursting in the cave of its mighty chest."

"And the giant retreated, promising never to return," I said.

"Aye," said Grandfather, pausing to set down his bowl and tamp tobacco into his pipe with the little finger of his right hand.

"Boru was a good king," Grandfather continued. His voice was musing, almost as though he talked to himself and not to me. He lit his pipe and began to puff it. "Boru wanted to hold his crown safe from the giant, and he wanted to keep Ireland free. Fomor wanted, from the depths of his greedy heart, to squander the wealth of this same great land and to enslave its brave people."

It seemed to me for a moment then that Grandfather was talking of Boru and Fomor and meaning something else entirely, and you should know that much of Boru's story became my own, though I was no high king. I was only Maggie, a girl of reddish hair and "very little common sense," as my brother Joe would have said.

And it was not all of Ireland, but only Shannon Farm that I wanted to hold on to. For the sake of

3

Grandfather, who was becoming ever more sad, and for Joe, whose labors in the field could not save us.

Against me stood, not Fomor, but Sir Henry Fitzhenry Drummond and the British—British laws, British rulers and, as you shall see, even British guns.

I didn't guess it in the beginning, not then, not when I was thirteen, three years ago, at my grandfather's knee, beside the hearth while we ate our morning porridge. I thought only we must have a horse to win The Galty Prize against the best flyers and jumpers in County Tipperary.

Brian Boru had known the name of his dire enemy, but my enemy was hidden from me. Men spoke of English misdeeds at Connory Mill and in dark cellars beneath city houses. Men were hounded and hanged for such talk. I know that now as well as I know the days are short in winter. But then I was unaware. If danger threatened, it was not mine. Not Maggie Shannon's danger. Then, I only sat breathlessly wanting another tale.

"It is to the honor of Boru and Ossian that the Galty steeplechase is run each year," I said, wanting the story of my father and his horse Tralee.

"Have I shown you the gold, Maggie?" Grandfather asked. His pale eyes brightened as he set his pipe upon the hearth and rose from the crooked chair.

He had brought out the gold coin before, but I followed him through the open doorway into his bedroom, eager to see it again.

Grandfather's bedroom was scarcely big enough to hold his narrow bed and lit only by light borrowed from the hearth. Behind us, in the room we had just left, turf logs glowed and hissed, their pungent aroma following us.

4

Together, Grandfather and I knelt on the hard-packed dirt floor in the corner of the room. He pried the coin from behind a loose stone in the wall while I watched for the first gleam of it.

"A guinea, Maggie, pure gold, saved back from the last time Shannons won The Galty."

Now the story was coming around to the time when my father was a young man.

"Brave horses and brave men ride every year for the prize," I said to keep the story going.

"And the bravest perhaps was your own father, Maggie. On his horse Tralee, he brought home the trophy twice."

"And you, also, have won the Galty twice, Grandfather."

"But neither of us could win the third time. Did I tell you? It takes three wins on the same horse for a rider to keep the trophy for all time. That has never happened."

"Three races—just like Boru and Ossian against the giant and the giant's horse."

Grandfather put the coin into my palm and squeezed my hand shut. The coin was heavy and colder than the stones that had hidden it. Its weight was as heavy as our need.

"The guinea is our fee for when next we have a horse to race. We must preserve it. We will not likely find another."

In profile, the face of a young Queen Victoria of England gazed serenely beyond the edge of the coin. The portrait hanging on my schoolroom wall showed her with an extra chin and a more burdensome crown.

"We'll have a horse again sometime," I said, believing that was the only way. "You'll see, Grandfather.

We'll win the Galty Prize. You'll set the trophy back where it belongs on our mantle shelf. With the bag of gold that goes with the trophy, we'll buy back Shannon Farm."

"That only Sir Henry Drummond can decide. He cannot be compelled to sell. It may not be enough." His voice was dreamy, but he had not disputed that we would get a horse and that we would win again. Part of him still believed.

"If one bag of gold isn't enough, then we'll race again—and a third time, if that's what it takes!" I said, a plan forming in my brain.

Grandfather's watery eyes looked, like the eyes of Queen Victoria, past the edges of today, and I knew he was seeing days long past, when he and my father had ridden to victories at the Galty before even my brother Joe was born. I wanted to hear again about those lost days.

"Like Boru and Ossian," I said. "Like you and my father and your fine horses."

"Like Boru for the crown of Tipperary," Grandfather whispered in his scratchy voice.

"And did the giant keep his promise never to return?"

"Ah, Maggie, my dear, even a giant must keep his promises. No, he never returned."

Joe's voice boomed from the doorway behind us. "And so now we have the British!"

I closed my hand tightly on the coin. I knew before I turned to look that his face would be as angry as his words.

"Better the giant," Joe said, "than Sir Henry Drummond, I'm thinking. Better honest labor than idle

6

dreams! Here the two of you are nattering over horses and races, times that will never come again."

"Joe, they will!" I shouted back at him. I would make it so.

Grandfather pried the coin from my hand, replaced it in the wall and sagged onto his bed.

Joe's voice had done that to Grandfather. I jumped up, ready to throw more angry words at my brother, but he was quicker.

"And that piece of gold!" he said, empty hands flung open before him. "Not even pennies roll through our door, and you hoard what could buy us a piglet or a hen, maybe even a calf."

"But it's our entry, Joe, for the Galty Chase," I said.

"And where is the horse? And who the rider? Those days are gone!" He dropped his hands, but still his palms were empty before him. "Famine gobbled up our horses and property and the rest of the gold. Famine and the cursed English chased most of Grandfather's family and friends into leaking boats bound for America. Many of them found only death at sea. Grandfather should be telling you that rather than feeding you a hash of nonsense!"

Joe's eyes were blue and mine were green, and the air between us became shot through with those colors, so intense were our feelings. Then it was his turn to sag. He leaned his young man's body against the doorjamb. Weary and muddy from a night in the barn, he buried his face in his cap for a moment. I feared he might be crying.

Joe crying was a thought that stabbed me hard, but finally, when he removed his cap, his eyes were dry, though red and smeared round with dirt.

"Oh, it's the curse of this land," Joe said. "I do apologize, Grandfather. Iris birthed her calf last night. It

7

didn't live." His voice was hollow with misery. He pushed a hand through his wild, dark hair, and I wanted to go to him and put my arms around him, but it wasn't our custom to be tender with each other.

Our dog Bran, who had spent the night in the barn with Joe, came wagging into the room and pushed a silvery muzzle into Grandfather's lap.

"And the old cow?" Grandfather swung his legs over the edge of the bed and sat, his hand resting between Bran's pointed ears.

"It's lucky we didn't lose Iris as well. She may still give us milk to supply the Big House." By which he meant Drummond's mansion, family, and the many servants living there. The milk was part of our rent. Our crops were due Sir Henry as well.

Joe had counted on the calf, a heifer that would eventually bring a calf of its own and maybe enough milk to sell after Drummond got his share. Or another bullock to trade for milling his portion of the grain from the new acres he was clearing for Drummond.

"We still have Daisy and her bullock," I said.

"And maybe Iris is not so old that she can't bring us a live calf next year," Joe said, but his eyes were nearly as sad as Grandfather's.

"We shouldn't have to wait for next year for something good to happen," I said, nearly spilling what I was planning into the air of the room.

"It's hard work that's needed on Shannon Farm if we are to win back our few acres, if we are to keep even the little we have. Finnerty and his family are the latest to find themselves without a roof for their cottage."

I shivered at the thought of the roof being torn from our own cottage while we watched, a sack of belongings

8

at our feet and nowhere to go but the road. I shivered, too, for my brother's sacrifices and misery.

Joe had given plenty of hard work to tilling and planting the land, with little result, and his labor was turning him sour and angry.

I lowered my eyes and went quickly to the hearth. My brother would have eaten no more than a cold potato while he saw Iris through her birthing. I ladled steaming stirabout into a bowl, an action that drew the dog's grave attention.

"I suppose you have fairy magic on your side?" Joe said, just as if he'd read my thoughts through my cast-down eyes. He took the bowl from my hand.

"If it takes fairy magic!" I said, then snapped my mouth shut tight. I would find a horse such as King Boru's to win the Galty Prize that is run each year in Boru's memory. A horse would save us. A horse would give Grandfather back what he had lost. The golden coins spilling over the lip of the trophy cup would bring back ownership of Shannon Farm and repair Grandfather's dwindling happiness. A horse would ease Joe's burden.

The plan that had begun in my head would lead me to triumph and then to disaster—though sometimes, looking back, I am not clear as to which of what happened was winning and which was losing. Agreeing with Joe, you might say I was too old to be plotting about fairies and leprechauns. You might be right, but still, that was my way at the time, and as with most matters, it is not always easy to identify the truth of things.

As I saw it then, I had no other way. I was ready to begin that very night.

⇥ CHAPTER 2 ⇤

THE FAIRY WOODS

I listened to my brother's breathing until it softened into sleep. Joe's pallet bed was only across the loft from mine, so I was careful as I slipped from bed—though I had little fear of Joe waking until morning, not after last night's vigil in the barn with Iris.

March in Ireland brings long days and short nights, and I had much to do in the midnight hours. Most of the day just past I'd spent preparing—gathering what I would need and finding the right place to dig. If Joe had not been so exhausted, he would have noticed chores undone and duties half finished.

I pulled on my dress, feeling in the dark to be sure I had it seam side out, which is a protection against fairies. I had listened often enough to Grandfather warn of the folk he called the "good people." I must not take chances.

"The good people," Grandfather often said. "We call them that to make them think we honor them. Never forget, they steal babes and even strong men—dogs and girls, too, likely—and they can cage your reason or cross your eyes."

When Grandfather was speaking so, Joe might argue against filling my head with fairy nonsense. "Stop with your daft talk," he would say. "Worry about whether we have potatoes enough for winter. Worry about what new ways the English might invent to drive us into the sea. Worry about Sir Henry buying sheep to replace us on our land, not fairy magic!"

So, Grandfather and I kept silent about fairies when Joe was near and prayed that he wouldn't come to grief for his disbelief in them.

I slipped down the ladder. Glad for the charm of my dress worn inside out, I tiptoed past Grandfather's open door. Bran left his rug by the hearth to pad along behind, and together we went toward the barn. Around us, the soft night seemed hardly to stir from our breathing and passing through it.

When we left the barn and closed the gate to our yard behind us, I was clasping a small bundle and a spade to my chest. In the darkness, I was glad for the slap of Bran's tail on my leg as my arms shivered with the evening chill and excitement for the adventure ahead. Throughout the long hike to the Fairy Woods, my mind galloped forward to the night's work I had planned.

At the edge of the woods, I stopped to catch my breath before going on. Grandfather's warnings sounded again in my ear, but I reminded myself that I was here to capture a leprechaun and make him give me a horse.

*****

I had first come to these woods with Grandfather to gather hazelnuts. Then, even with the sun shining fiercely, I had felt chilled as we looked into stone cairns that were bare, windowless rooms tucked into the roots of giant yew trees.

"Built by Druids who lived here when Ireland was young—though the trees were already ancient," Grandfather had told me.

As houses, they would have barely fit a child, and I could not have stood in one without stooping. When I said so, Grandfather answered with a whisper. "And so they suit the fairy folk just right. It's why they favor this place."

I was glad that day with Grandfather to leave the woods with its feeling of the evil magic he told me the ancient Druids had practiced. I avoided returning until yesterday morning when I slipped away to visit the woods and find the best location for my trap.

The place had frightened me even more than before. It had been all I could do to walk through it in broad daylight.

Now I was back despite my fears—and in the dark, too. The sight of Grandfather sagging onto the bed and the sound of frustration in Joe's voice spurred me. I must change their lives and mine.

Above, the moon slipped in and out among the clouds, no more than a sliver, giving less light than a distant star. Yet, light was caught up in the mists that swirled ankle deep on the forest floor and rose in columns like dim ghosts brushing my arms and cheeks with clammy fingers.

I peered into those mists, thinking I saw will-o-the-wisps, those bobbing lanterns held by fairy hands. I closed my ears to the enchantment of fairy piping and closed my eyes to the lights. I mustn't be led skipping and dancing against reason, following such lights and sounds into the waters of the River Tar to drown like the little O'Malley girl had done when Grandfather was a lad.

Bran bounded ahead into the woods. I pulled myself away from the will-o-the-wisps and after the dog, into the shadows of the oaks and yews. The horse . . . I must think only of the grand horse. The horse would be worth the fear and the danger.

"Such a horse . . . to win the prize again . . . it would be worth a man's life," Grandfather had said.

I went deeper into the woods along a path I had chosen yesterday, past stones piled on stones, wondering whose blood had made the dark stains on these ancient Druid altars. Young girls like myself, perhaps, with their wrists staked and ankles tied. I hurried past, feeling misty fingers on my skin.

We stopped in a clearing beneath the outstretched arm of a giant oak. "This is the place," I whispered, both to Bran and against the silence of the forest.

I dropped my bundle beside the tree's stout trunk and fell to work with the spade, scooping shovelful after shovelful of the spongy earth until a pit had begun to take shape. Bran put his own paws to the digging whenever I took a moment's rest. It's only like hoeing potatoes, I thought. But my shoulders and back ached long before I had dug deep enough to be sure a leprechaun couldn't struggle from the pit once he had fallen in.

Dig, I thought, and don't mind the spriggins and phookas and hags, the fairy folk I felt ranked against me behind the clustered thorn and elder at the edge of the clearing. They were watchers who would wish me no good fortune. If they saw fear, they might come at me

13

with shrieks, and fingernails to tear my skin. I brushed the hair from my forehead and fell to my task.

As if he, too, sensed the sentries who guarded these woods, Bran began to whine and worry.

"It's all right, Bran," I said. "I'li soon be done."

And soon I was—weaving branches over the open pit and tossing twigs and leaves to disguise the trap. Then I spread open my bundle, touching each of its contents with trembling hands before selecting a small pouch of tobacco. With this I baited my trap, opening the pouch slightly, so its pungent odor could waft to a leprechaun nose. I placed the pouch on the fragile roof of the pit and, beside it, a jug of whiskey carefully mixed with honey and milk. I regretted the theft of Grandfather's whiskey and tobacco, but he would be glad when I brought home the horse.

Stopping for a moment to admire my handiwork, I retreated to the bushes and knelt to watch, keeping Bran near.

The moon, such as it was, put itself behind the fullest branches of the trees, and I could see only the dog's yellow eyes. I heard a dry cough close by, the bark of a fox, and feared Bran might leave me to give chase, but the dog only whined.

"Hush," I said, and he lay still, the two of us crouching, quiet as shadows.

We waited. The silence deepened and, also, the dark. Cold pressed heavy hands against my shoulders. I shivered, my heart pounded, and I shrank closer to Bran for his warmth. I wanted to hug him and say words that would encourage us both, but I must do nothing to warn a leprechaun that we were there.

Sometimes the moon broke from behind a cloud to show the untouched bait, and sometimes the air stirred windlessly as if spirits of the Druids moved about. Bran huddled close as I rehearsed my plan.

A leprechaun would find the bait and fall through the branches and twigs into the pit. He'd cry and threaten and beg with fairy cunning to be pulled up. And, finally, when he saw I'd never bend, he'd be forced to give me what I wanted. I would have a horse to win the Galty Prize for three years' runnings, three wins to make the trophy ours to keep, with coins enough to let Joe buy back the farm.

At that moment, Bran stiffened against my knee, and I felt the beginning rumble of his growl. Something moved in the clearing. Then even the dim light that showed the movement was gone. The cold grew until I felt it to the marrow of my bones.

Bran lifted his head to howl, but his voice was lost as another howl, louder and deeper than his, filled the clearing with its sound. The howl beat at us from all sides, with screeches that carried the cold with it, wrapping us in icy currents.

A fairy storm leaped with menace from the pit in a misty whirl, bringing its own cold light. Chilling clouds reached out to my hiding place and pulled me to my feet. Crystal rain, knives and needles, drove at me through the trees, freezing my heart. The wind plucked at the harp strings of my hair, lightning cracked, and thunder roared while the trees thrashed their limbs and groaned. Through it all, I heard a wild voice cry, "A penny for the horse."

"A penny for the horse." The voice cackled and braided itself into the confusion of screaming storm and wailing trees.

"Bran," I called, my words twisting with the other sounds. "Bran!" I couldn't see, but tried desperately to find the shape of him through the storm.

The dog brushed my leg, rough and bristling fur against the storm's fury, warmth against chill. I fought the storm to go down on hands and knees beside him, clutching his rough coat with one hand and holding to the ground with the other to anchor myself. I shut my eyes while the icy blasts rocked me and whipped my hair.

Then, as if it had been a fire smothered by a blanket, the storm vanished. It coiled from the ground at my feet into the sky with a fierceness that broke the clouds and rolled them back. The moon was a pale grin against the sooty sky.

I rose to my knees, my hands still balled from clutching Bran and the forest floor.

All was quiet. The shapes of the trees were outlined vividly, so still, after their wild thrashing, that I thought all had turned to stone—trees, grass and fern. The hush was so deep that I did not know whether to fear the silence or fear more that it would end. I dared not breathe.

Gradually, a stirring began around me, the natural movement of air on the hairs of my arms and Bran's breath on my ankles. In my palm was the shape and burn of a coin. How it had come into my hand I had no idea, unless I had scooped it up, along with moldering leaves and soil from the forest floor. I let out a breath as I fingered the coin's smooth edges in wonder, straining to catch a gleam of it in the moonlight.

Then, without warning, Bran launched himself into an attack. He hurtled by me with a force that threw me onto my side.

Struggling to get up, I could see the blur of Bran. He wrestled with a creature I couldn't see, though I heard it grunting and growling. Then the thing crashed in retreat through brambles and trees with Bran in pursuit.

I rose and called the dog back, brushing at myself with palms that I suddenly realized were as empty as the giant, Fomor's, heart. The coin was gone, dropped from my hands when Bran knocked into me.

Frantically, I searched in the midnight black, the moon once more gone behind a cloud. The voice from the storm had promised, "A penny for a horse! A penny for a horse!" Had I really heard that? Had I really held a coin in my hand?

Bran returned and sniffed the ground, but for all his help, as I scratched through the leaves, the coin remained lost, maybe forever.

We returned to the cottage, cold and wet. Tomorrow by daylight, I would return. I must find the coin.

⊰ CHAPTER 3 ⊱

UNDER THE ROWAN TREE

I pulled myself from bed, coming awake weary and sick at heart, with Joe already dressed and scolding me for sleeping past cockcrow. I thanked heaven he had no way of knowing that cock had welcomed the first light of day only a few hours after I had crept up the ladder to the loft and slid into bed.

As I pulled on my dress, I was glad I had worn it seam-side-out the night before. The proper side didn't show the signs of last night's labors, even though the grime of the inside clung to my skin. The dress was still wet, but with a dry apron, maybe no one would notice. I would wear my shawl to hide the scratches and bruises from my struggle with the storm.

"I'll be right down, Joe," I said. "I slept poorly last night, with dreams waking me through the hours." I rubbed the sand from my eyes and yawned.

"As if you didn't dream enough through the day," Joe said, going down the ladder ahead of me. "Nonsense about horse races, I'd wager." But his voice was gentle, without the edge of irritation I'd heard yesterday.

When I joined my brother downstairs, Grandfather had the fire aglow and the breakfast porridge heating. Noontime potatoes roasted in the ashes on the hearth. Wooden bowls sat on the dresser, waiting to be filled. The quarrelsome sounds of hens came from the yard, and the cows lamented from their shed. Even old Bridey could be heard whinnying.

"I'll get to my milking, Grandfather," Joe said from the doorway. "You can send Maggie with my stirabout when it's hot."

I poked at the fire. "Grandfather," I said, "do you think Iris will have milk after losing her calf?"

"We can but hope, Maggie, love. She is an old cow. At least we still have Daisy and her fine bullock. I had hoped we might have been able to keep him for butchering—meat for us and some to share." He began to fill the wooden bowls with porridge. "But I suppose now he must go to Drummond for rent in place of the stillborn—of course, he might bring a bit extra, if Sir Henry feels generous."

"It's not fair that everything goes to Drummond." I took a bowl from Grandfather's hand. "Not just our grain and meat, but everything good in the townland."

Grandfather nodded. He put his spoon to his stirabout.

"We'll get the money to buy back the land. Things cannot always go wrong."

"Money, child? If we had money we could buy the world."

19

I finished eating and left the fire to return my bowl to the dresser and fetch one for Joe, who would be waiting for it in the barn. I stood for a moment with my hand resting on the shelf of the giant piece of furniture. It had come into the room in some past time of prosperity and never been sold. My mother must have loved it and my mother's mother before. I wished I could know the long-ago woman who had first owned it, who had pointed a finger and said, "There, there is where I want it to stand." I traced my fingers over its silky surface and the feel of the slick coin came back to me, the coin from the Fairy Woods.

Maybe I could persuade Joe to let me work in his field, the one Drummond was letting him clear for rye. It would be easy to get to the Fairy Woods from there.

I dished porridge from the great potful that Grandfather had cooked, then went to find Joe.

"While you take the milk to Drummond's," I said, the bowl warm in my hands, "I could start clearing the new acres in that high pasture for you." I prayed that Joe would let me go.

Joe looked up from his milking, his hands strong and firm on Daisy's teats. "As it happens, Drummond's groom will be returning from market in Cahir. He'll stop here on his way home and pick up the milk himself," Joe answered. He stood and took the bowl I offered.

"But I could still clear the field for you," I said. "You could have the day to repair the shed. You said you've been looking for such a day."

"Clear the field, will you? And when would you be finished with such a project? When my beard is white and you have lost your teeth, I imagine."

"Please, Joe, I could begin."

20

"As it happens, you will take the cows to pasture, relieving Grandfather to stay home. The shed can wait for a rainy day, and I can move more stones in an hour than you can move in a week."

Taking the cows to pasture was a job Joe did not often trust to me. Another day I would have been glad for the responsibility. But now I was disappointed. The pasture was near the Fairy Woods, it was true, but Joe would be working between those woods and me.

He finished the milking and saw me through the gate with the two cows, the bullock, and Bran. "I'll be along soon with Bridey," he said. "You be sure to watch the bullock doesn't wander to Drummond's woodlot. I don't want him to get scratched or turn an ankle."

I understood well enough that I must keep the animals from wandering. I would not dare leave them.

But once in the pasture, with Bran minding the cows, the Fairy Woods began to call. I sat beneath a rowan tree, its branches ready to burst with leaves and showy blossoms. Below me was the narrow woodlot and beyond it Drummond's fields of rye. Above me was a hillock. Over the hillock, Joe would be working. I stood and reached into the tree to pluck a small twig. A rowan branch was a guard against fairy magic, just like last night's wearing of a dress seam-side-out. I rolled the rough wood between my fingers and tucked it into my apron pocket.

Glancing back to Bran crouching between the cows and the woodlot, I made my way up the hill. At the top, I hid behind a tumble of stones, someone's long ruined wall, and watched.

Joe was using his mattock to pry stones from the stubborn earth, reaching toward the unused acres to make them productive, to keep square with Drummond rents. Joe seldom spoke of buying back the farm. But that, of course, was what he wanted even though he hedged it round with scoffs whenever I spoke of the same dream in terms of horses and trophy cups.

Joe lifted stones onto his barrow to cart them to the wall he was building. The wall was like other walls, not built to keep anything from getting in or out of the field but somewhere to put the stones of the Irish earth. I had often heard Joe say, "It's as if the rocks grow of themselves, pushing up time and again through the ages to spoil an Irishman's plans."

Was it worth the struggle? Joe would say the land was worth any price you had to pay. Never mind that others had broken backs and hearts, he would work to make life different for himself.

I turned my back on Joe and leaned against the tumbled wall. How could I get by him? Below, lay the road to Cahir. Last night's fairy storm had mucked up the woods where I had labored, but not even dampened the road.

As I pondered the road and the storm, red and gold Gypsy wagons jolted into view. An odd assortment of donkeys and nags pulled the wagons, and a string of scraggly ponies and horses followed. Children ran back and forth between the wagons, scattering dust.

"Tinkers!" Grandfather called such Gypsy folk, and I knew he said the word with contempt. But the free laughter that drifted from the road rang out like gold. Brightly colored skirts flared from the waists of women perched on the back steps of the wagons. Where had they been and where were they going? Did Gypsy women dream of a cottage and land of their own? Did the children yearn for school and books? I did not envy their life always on the move, but it might be fine to go with

22

them for a while and see more of the countryside than the few miles I knew.

While I strained to understand the strange language, Romany, that I heard as the Gypsies rattled nearer, I caught the drum of a galloping horse coming from the opposite direction as the caravan. I thrilled as a black stallion started up the hill toward Joe's pasture, its tail flagged and its hooves dancing across the rocky ground. It was Cashel, surely!

The horse that had won last year's Galty Race for the Connorys took the hill with no less than Patrick Connory seated on its strong, glossy back.

Grandfather said no finer horse paced the county than Cashel and no better horseman lived than Patrick Connory. "The two remind me of myself and my own horse, Seaneen," he had once told me and had gone on to describe the past, long before the famine. Then he had said, "No, they are more like your father when he was a youth on his fine mare, Erin's Girl, the pair of them racing to no less than two Galty wins. One more and the trophy would have been ours to keep forever."

When Patrick reached Joe, my brother stopped work, using his mattock as a prop for his gangly form.

Patrick, Joe's childhood friend, had grown to be as handsome as a prince, with thick brown hair and fine, muscular shoulders. He pulled Cashel up and kept the dancing horse in place as he leaned from the saddle to speak to Joe.

What was he saying? Some said that men gathered at the Connory mill to talk of a free Ireland. Talk like that was dangerous in a land of English soldiers and spies. Joe always said that he didn't have time for politics. But he admired Patrick and Patrick's father and sometimes went to the mill when Patrick was home.

23

Joe dropped his mattock and fetched Bridey, climbing onto the old mare's bare back. Together they left the field and took the road toward Connory Mill.

I couldn't believe what I'd just seen! The way to the woods was clear. Surely, I was meant to go there and find the coin. And maybe the Gypsies had horses to sell. Was there, perhaps a horse behind those Gypsy wagons? A horse to be bought for a leprechaun's penny?

I looked hard at the animals, Iris, Daisy and her bullock, their necks bent to their grazing, Bran keeping watch. I ran for the woods.

⊰ CHAPTER 4 ⊱

A LEPRECHAUN'S PENNY

In the woods, no sign remained of last night's storm, other than a damp smell coming off the leaves of the trees and a greater sponginess to the ground. By daylight, the cairns and altars of the ancient Druids were only cunning homes and piles of stone. The clumps of thorn no longer hid malicious watchers. Only the pit showed the fury of the wind and rain.

Limbs and briars filled the hole nearly to the top. Green leaves ripped from their branches littered the ground. At least I hadn't dreamed the storm, and if not the storm then not the voice or the coin. I sifted leaves until my fingers were prickly and brown with dirt. A coin must be in the dirt somewhere. My labor must count for more than torn fingernails and bloody knuckles.

Pulling debris from the pit, twig by twig and clod by clod, I found nothing. But there had been a coin! I had held it in my hand and known it was the reward for all my efforts. I searched on, disregarding my torn and bruised hands. A difference in the air told me that afternoon had faded. My shoulders sagged and my chin dropped forward to my chest.

Must I give up? As I scuffed through the leaves beyond the pit, a dull gleam caught my eye, then winked out. Frantically, I threw myself to my knees, once more searching for the coin.

My fingers found it before my eyes. Feeling its roundness along with the dirt I scooped into my palm, I clutched it to my chest. Then, opening my fist in wonder, I rolled the coin over and over and caressed its worn surfaces and edges.

"It's the promise of a horse," I said.

It wasn't gold, but just the same, it felt warm and alive. With trembling fingers, I dropped it into my apron pocket with the rowan twig and hurried back to the cows. I had been gone a long time.

I ran across Joe's field and up the sides of the hillock. As I reached the top, I heard Bran barking. Scrambling over the tumbled wall, I caught sight of the dog heading off Iris, keeping her from entering the woodlot and, beyond that, Drummond's field of rye. Where were the other animals?

Praying they were safe and had done no damage to themselves, I crossed into the woodlot, my heart hammering as I ran. Emerging from the woods, I spotted first Daisy and then her calf.

They had turned Drummond's field to shambles. The rye, where it was still standing, had grown to the span of a palm, little more, but most of it lay crushed and broken.

"Wicked cows!" I shouted and ran toward Daisy. "You've ruined the grain!"

Bran barked at the cow's heels and Daisy trotted away from him into a stand of still untrodden rye. Her thick hooves crushed the stalks, and the bullock followed clumsily, trampling more tender shoots and lowing in confusion. Together they stumbled over wet ground where the mud sucked at their feet and created a mire of drowned and broken rye.

Bran cut across the bullock's path, turning him back, but more plants were lost as the animals trotted along, scything with their hooves as they went.

Then Sir Henry Drummond himself appeared in front of me—a giant of a man with a slate-gray beard, astride a towering gray horse.

"You are the Shannon girl," he said, as if he were pronouncing a judgment upon me.

"I'm Maggie, sir," I answered, nodding, praying for the scene of ruin to disappear.

Sir Henry leaned toward me from the gray horse. "Now tell me how this disaster happened."

It was the cows . . . Daisy, Iris, and the calf. I left them for just the wink of an eye. I had to . . . "

"Left them, girl? Left them, you say? Surely your grandfather gave you instructions to stay close by?"

"Just for a moment, sir. I thought it would be all right."

Sir Henry scrubbed at his beard with irritation showing in his eyes. "Evidently, you were wrong," he said. "I shall inspect the damage. Tell your grandfather that I will see him for an accounting. These are hard times, as you know, and I have an estate in England, as well as this barony, to keep up. I must be compensated for the loss of a cash crop."

"Yes, sir. I'm sorry." I shivered, cold as I had been the night before in the Fairy Woods. Then I picked up the rope again and led Daisy back through the woodlot to where Iris was watching, her eyes huge and questioning.

Look at the price I'd paid! And the price Grandfather and Joe must pay for my scheming. For one single penny!

As I followed the cows and Bran home, the sky softened and began to rain. The coin in my pocket no longer felt warm and alive between my fingers, but cold and dead. How could I explain to Grandfather? What would I tell Joe?

⊰ CHAPTER 5 ⊱

THE RUINED FIELD

In the cottage, I found Grandfather dozing by the fire. I sat for a time without waking him, but finally I was so lonely in my misery that I shook him gently and told the story of the ruined field.

"I left them to go to the Fairy Woods, Grandfather," I finished. "Remembering the time you took me there, I wanted to see them again." It wasn't much of the truth. How could I tell him more?

Grandfather wrung his hands in anguish. I had meant to give him joy, but I had set misery on his face and in his heart.

"Maggie, Maggie," he said, "the woods, the Fairy Woods. Didn't I tell you to beware them? And the cows, Maggie, the cows and the bullock . . . to leave them as you did. We had only a shred of hope left, that calf, and . . . "

I hung my head. "I thought I could get a horse from one of the little men with their stores of gold and promises."

I would have called back my words if I could. The tale would have to be told someday, but I wasn't ready just yet.

"Gold and promises, gold and promises," echoed Grandfather, rocking his body forward and back on his chair by the fire. "It's not your fault, but mine. I led you into this with my tales. Joe was right to discourage me. It's my fault, but I fear we must all pay up." He continued to rock. "And the field, Maggie?" he said. "How bad was it?"

My throat felt clogged with dust as I described the field. "Sir Henry said we must make up for the damage."

"What will become of us, Maggie? What price will he put on the field? What will your brother say?"

"Perhaps Sir Henry will forgive us, Grandfather. Drummond House has many fields and collects the produce of a great barony. Surely . . . "

Grandfather spat at the fire. "Hush, Maggie! The landlords dished soup to starving tenants when the potatoes failed. Then they took our lands and horses. As they took all lands and horses in the townland—save only those of the Connorys who had the blessing of owning a mill to grind Drummond grain."

The speech had been a greater one than I had ever heard from Grandfather, and the words cut deeply. I was shivering with shame and fear when Joe walked in, returning from wherever he had gone with Patrick Connory.

Repeating the tale to my brother, whose face turned from disbelief to anger and frustration, was harder than the task of digging the leprechaun trap.

"He will take the cows!" Joe said. "He will take Daisy and Iris, and little by little our livelihood will go. Like the Finnertys, we'll be thrown from our lands and the green pastures given to sheep!"

The next day, Joe went to Drummond and heard his accounting while I waited with Grandfather, fearing the worst. Grandfather was sunk in memories, I knew, for he sat and muttered the names of my father and his own sisters and brother, dead or gone to America.

The dread was so heavy by the time Joe returned that I had already imagined Joe, Grandfather, and myself left with only small bundles and a few potatoes. Would we live like tinkers always on the move? Like the poor Finnertys, would we live in an overturned wagon? Would we beg to keep ourselves alive?

But, in the end, it was not the cows that went, but the precious bullock that would have put us some ahead.

"First, Iris's calf dropped stillborn, and now the bullock gone," Joe said. "It could be worse, I suppose. We could have lost the cows and their milk. Perhaps the new pasture will bring us in something extra when it's cleared and planted." But his voice lacked the sound of belief. He collapsed onto a stool, pain building on his face.

"It isn't you, Maggie, I blame, so much as the damn landlords!" he said. "Surely, God in His goodness did not place Irishmen on His greenest isle to be always near starvation and in debt to strangers. Golden grain ripens at harvest, sheep and cattle munch the rich grass, but only potatoes fill our plates. Only across the sea in England do they taste the sweetness of Tipperary lamb, beef, and vegetables."

Joe crashed his fist onto the table, but his words shocked me more than the fist, words I had never heard from Joe or Grandfather. I had overheard whispers

31

muttered when I passed men, two or three with their donkey carts taking milk to the Big Houses, three or four lounging at the mill after delivering their grain. I knew without being told that the danger of English guns lurked in every syllable.

Joe's words and the words of others accompanied me as I haltered the bullock and led him down the dusty road toward Drummond House. Brendan Connory had often told me that his brother Patrick and others were working for a free Ireland. Centuries of such work had done "precious little good and often brought grief," Joe had said when I told him. Now Joe himself had uttered treason.

In the English school, the teacher taught lessons of the might of the British Empire, naval heroes, and battles. What could Irish talk of parliaments, land reform and Irish independence do against such strength?

Joe often said that the Connory boys might have time to think of such things, but he had too much just to keep Shannon Farm from falling behind in rent. He would leave the "chasing of will-o-the-wisps to the poets, of which Ireland has a plenty." Did my brother still feel that way? The sight of him riding away from his pasture on old Bridey came to my mind, and I thought he'd been spending more time at the mill than he used to. Maybe Nan Connory's blue eyes and black hair weren't the only reasons he went to Patrick's house. I would ask my friend, Brendan. Brendan would know and might tell me.

I walked the bullock down the high middle of the wheel-rutted road. Neither of us was eager, but we were steady, and the great iron gates of Drummond House soon loomed before us, gates set between huge stone piers with tops on them like polished boulders. The gates of Troy could not have been so grand.

32

"One day I will ride through these gates on a champion horse, just like my father and grandfather." I said the words aloud to the bullock as if a pledge to him might make it so. "Not Sir Henry Fitzhenry Drummond nor Queen Victoria nor the devil himself shall prevent me." I thrust a fist into my apron pocket. The edge of the fairy coin bit hard into my knuckles.

⊰ CHAPTER 6 ⊱

THE GYPSY MARE

Riding his bay gelding, Sultan, Brendan Connory caught up to me on my way back to Shannon Farm. I looked up into his clear blue Connory eyes and read his concern. His nearly black Connory hair framed his face with damp curls. At sixteen, he had not yet attained his father's or his older brother Patrick's stature, but he had already grown into the Connory demeanor. He held himself straight in his saddle and controlled his mount with a strong and steady hand. I, who had never seen a prince before seeing Patrick Connory yesterday, now was acquainted with two!

"I heard of your terrible misfortune, Maggie," Brendan said, removing his cap as a gentleman might to a lady.

"News travels with the hounds when it's bad." I put a hand to Sultan's warm neck. Brendan's courtly gesture had brought a blush to my cheeks.

"You'll make up for it. The landlords cannot always take what they want for little cause. The rye in Sir Henry's field did not come there by his own labor or deserving of it."

His words hit me at a slant and chased the fire from my cheeks and put it in my heart.

"Brendan, tell me what the men say at the mill? Is it treason that's spoken of?"

"What do you know of treason, Maggie?"

"Joe said something, much like what you said about Sir Henry just now. It frightened me."

Brendan looked to the hills, his mouth a narrow line.

"Is this about driving the English out?" I asked.

"It is about Irish land for Irishmen and laws we make ourselves."

"This year I will win the Galty Prize. With the prize money, I'll buy back Shannon Farm."

Brendan continued to gaze for a moment longer at the hills, and I thought he hadn't heard me. Then he turned his face back to me, the snap of humor in his eyes. "A horse you'll be needing then!" he said. "Do you hear that, Sultan? Maggie Shannon plans to bring us ruin! You and me and also my brother Patrick and his great horse Cashel!" His laughter rang on the quiet air.

"I know it sounds daft for me to say it, Brendan. But I know. I just know that with the right horse and Grandfather to teach me . . . " I broke off, fearing he'd never understand.

But somehow he had understood, for his words became softer.

"Well, the tinkers are camped down by the river with a string of horses to trade for coin. Do you have any money, Maggie? A tinker trader will not part with a horse except for brass."

"It happens I do." I longed to tell him about the night in the woods and the coin. "Brendan, please."

"Ah, well," he said with devilment in his eyes and the corners of his mouth. "It's for Joe I'd be doing it then. Only for Joe, and you begging me so hard." He offered his hand and, placing my bare foot upon his boot in the stirrup, I climbed up behind him.

I was glad to be riding up to the Gypsy camp on a fine-looking horse, behind a fine-looking young man with boots on his feet and a jacket to keep off the chill. I wasn't coming as a poor peasant girl.

The Gypsy camp lay downstream from where I stood with Brendan on the bridge, I at the rail and Brendan a step back, holding Sultan's reins as the horse pranced, excited by the nearness of other animals.

"They're the very ones I saw on the road yesterday," I said, taking in the scarlet and gold wagons and the horses.

A trader was just now gathering his unshod ponies and horses into a string as the camp began to break up. The bright-skirted women plucked clothing from thorny gorse bushes where it had been put to dry. Boys ran after horses in a field that was a scramble of sheaf-like tails, rippling grain, and waving arms.

My own chase in Sir Henry's rye came to mind. I doubted the Gypsy boys were much concerned with the havoc they created in the pasture. They would soon be off to ruin another farmer's oats before any landlord caught up to them.

"I want to see the horses close up," I said. The hair on my arms rose in anticipation as I started toward the wagons.

Brendan followed, down to where the trader was haltering a spotted pony. The trader had his back to us, but I noted his black, slouched hat, the full sleeves of his collarless shirt, also his soft, scuffed boots.

"Are you after selling those horses, mister?" I asked him.

He turned then, revealing a young, beardless face and dark blue eyes. "And what do you think a trader would be doing? Is it that pitiful nag you wish to trade?" He nodded toward Brendan's sleek and dancing Sultan and said something in another language to the spotted pony.

"My friend's horse isn't for sale," I said. "It's I who have a mind to buy." My hand closed into a fist around the coin in my pocket.

The trader laughed outright. "Well then, perhaps yonder sturdy nag will do."

I looked at the ancient bowed neck of the mare the trader pointed to and shook my head. "She's old and worn out. I must have a horse that is young and strong."

"Don't be so hasty. See this fine horse," the trader said, indicating a glossy black pony. "This one is fine . . . he has a particularly fine temper."

I jumped as the pony showed ugly yellow teeth and laid back his ears in warning.

"Let's be gone, Maggie," Brendan said. "He's only jesting."

"I've come to buy."

The trader went on with his charade. "Or how about this beast?" he said, patting a swaybacked cob with a torn ear.

"You're teasing me, I know," I said. "But I have coin, and I will have none of these."

37

Rubbing his chin, the trader turned thoughtful. "Oh, I know," he said. "I have just the horse. A gallant mare, this one."

I heard a hoof rustle in the nearby grass and turned to sight the loveliest mare I had ever set eyes on. The red mane was tangled and the sides dusty and uncurried, but she stood tall, power rippling through her graceful body. Her tail flicked a fly from a perfect haunch, and when she turned to look at me, her ears pricked forward, her eyes filling with intelligent, questioning warmth. She nickered softy, a message just for me. My heart went soft.

"Why didn't you show me this horse first?" It was all I could do to keep from throwing my arms around the horse's neck.

The mare reached her muzzle forward and nickered again. The nicker echoed the leprechaun's promise. I could hear it.

I placed my palm against the velvet muzzle, praying for the moment not to go away. I looked to the trader.

"Quite a beauty this one," the trader said, shaking his head. "But no good to me. With that lame foot she's little better than a pot of glue, so slow she is. Why, I'll let you have her for a leprechaun's penny!" He laughed at the joke he'd made.

From behind me, Brendan said, "Maggie, let's go. We've heard enough of his jests." Sultan blew through his nostrils and stamped.

My breath stopped. "A leprechaun's penny!" My eyes saw only the mare silhouetted in dazzling sunlight, but the sight in my mind was of myself, mounted on the brave creature, sailing over logs and fences and stone walls as I led the hunters in the Galty Cup Chase.

Slowly, looking the trader in the eye, I stood tall, drew my fist from my pocket and opened it. The coin glowed darkly in my palm.

The trader stepped back and looked at the coin. Shock was written on his leathery face. He shrugged, then laughed.

"For a penny, then," he said, whisking the coin from my palm with two fingers. He held it briefly in front of one eye, and I, too, looked at the odd markings. Maybe the thing was truly a leprechaun's penny, truly worth the price of the mare.

"You have beaten me at my joke. This hide and these bones are yours." The trader laughed as though the joke was really on me. "If you treat her right, she'll trot you to town one day."

"I have more plans for her than that! What name is she called?"

"Call her what you like," he said and shoved the mare's rope into my hand, then returned to his business of haltering the other horses.

I touched the velvet muzzle once more, and the mare turned, showing a blazed left hind leg. The blaze, white and beautiful of itself, ran down to meet a parchment-colored hoof, cocked to keep weight from it. An ugly crack split the hoof from bottom nearly to top.

"You're hurting," I cried, clapping a hand to my mouth. "Poor darling. Poor darling!" The hurt swelled, not only the ankle above the hoof, but my own heart as well.

"Oh, Maggie," Brendan said. He went quickly onto his knees, touching the hoof, feeling the ankle to where the leg reached the hoof at the pastern. "It's bad, Maggie. It's very bad. The horse is not fit to walk, let alone run. I fear Joe will be plenty sore at me for all this. Truly it's a curse all right—that's what you've bought."

"Can't we fix it?"

"We had a horse at the mill once who threw a shoe and split its hoof, not so bad as this one, I recall. My father had a terrible time. The hoof collected pus, and the ankle swelled so that the horse nearly died with fever. After that the horse was never the same, never seemed strong. When the hoof cracked a second time, we had the poor thing put down."

"That won't happen to this mare," I said. "She's young and strong—see the fine muscles that play beneath her hide, see her strong bones and her powerful neck. She'll be good as new by race time." Couldn't Brendan understand the mare was magical?

"You mustn't count on it. The hoof is very bad. I doubt she'll run at all. And she'll never be a match for the great horses of Tipperary."

I looked from the ankle to the mare's deep eyes. She pushed her muzzle against my cheek, the velvet thrilling me to my toes. I placed my hand on the lovely neck. "You're the one," I said. "I know you're the one."

So, Brendan put me on his horse again. We made our way slowly home, the mare taking her time and lifting her sore foot every step of the way, hobbling home. Joe and Grandfather would think me a foolish, brainless girl. Two days before I had to explain a ruined field they counted on and now, this scruffy, limping horse.

Looking backward from Brendan's saddle, I told the mare again, "You're the one."

The mare looked up and bobbed her head, almost as though saying "yes." Almost a promise.

⊰ CHAPTER 7 ⊱

A FAVOR OF THE HOOF

W hen we reached the mill, Brendan stopped. "I'm sorry I can't go the rest of the way with you, Maggie, but my brother, Patrick, is home, and I promised him some time."

"It's all right, Brendan. Thank you for taking me to the tinker camp. I'll never forget."

"It's not 'forget' that worries me, Maggie. More like 'forgive.' I hope you won't be sorry later on."

"Hush, now. Don't worry. The mare will be fine. Really."

Brendan dismounted and helped me. His hands at my waist guided my slide from behind the cantle of the saddle to the ground, where I stood waiting for him to release me. It was almost as if he'd forgotten the simple job of opening his hands.

When he did let go of me, his eyes held me where I was for a moment longer. "Maggie, when you can, come by the mill to see my mother. She's always asking after you. We all care for you. I'll help you if I can."

"I'll come by," I told him. "Thank her kindly for thinking of me . . . and thank you, too, Brendan . . . for your words."

Only then did Brendan swing himself back into the saddle. We said goodbye, and Brendan galloped Sultan down the road to the mill where his brother would be waiting. Immediately I missed him standing beside me. I missed his comfort.

I started the mare walking again, keeping myself close enough to take in the good horse smell. I shivered with pleasure each time the velvet nose pushed into my arm. Grandfather, too, would hear the heart messages that came to me from the mare, reassuring and wise. His eyes, when he saw her, would reflect my own joy.

As I topped the rise in the road near Shannon Farm, leading the mare, I saw Grandfather in the yard between the cottage and the shed. He had brought my little stool, my creepie, out of doors to sit in the fine spring sunshine to mend Joe's socks, and I knew that he had seen me, although he didn't get up. Only hours before, I had left him, taking our only bullock to Drummond House. Did he recognize that it was me returning with this beautiful horse? How could he imagine such a change in fortune?

As I approached, Grandfather stood, peered more closely, and hurried stiff-legged to the gate. His dear, freckled face reflected the wonder he must have felt.

"Maggie," he said. "Is it you?"

I led the mare to him and stood back while he took the rope.

He ran his hand down her neck and over her withers. He quickly scanned her lines with appreciation, his practiced eyes glowing.

"My, my, she is surely a beauty." Though his voice had filled with excitement, he still wouldn't have guessed the mare belonged to us.

When he noted the cracked hoof, he clucked and said, "I see she favors that foot. What a pity to see an injury in the likes of a mare such as this one. Did you find her on the road? I've never seen her about. She's unshod. Maybe the tinkers left her behind."

I placed my hand on Grandfather's arm. "She's ours. I bought her. She will win the Galty Prize. She'll bring us back Shannon Farm."

Grandfather's expression mingled disbelief with wonder and, perhaps, hope. "No, no, Maggie. It's not possible. And she's beautiful, but . . . "

"I bought her with a leprechaun's penny, Grandfather. I've been given a sign that she will win."

"Leprechaun, Maggie? What leprechaun?" He pushed me back so he could read my face. "How did you come by this mare? What are you prating of, girl? What do you mean?"

I told him all of it—the parts I'd omitted the day before—of digging the trap and baiting it, of the terrible storm and the coin, of the Gypsy's jest and the bargain. "Oh, Grandfather, she is good. Isn't she?"

"Leprechauns, Maggie? The little people? Haven't I warned you enough?" He struck the side of his head with his hand. "Don't you know they never give anything free of pain? I fear for us all." Again he struck his head and continued his muttering.

43

Finally, he returned his attention to the mare. He circled, measuring, assessing. He ran his fingers over every inch of her and looked deep into her eyes.

The mare allowed him, and when he finished, she nudged his arm. She was pure trust as well as pure beauty.

"She is grand, Maggie," he said. "I agree."

He paused and considered her again, one finger pursing his mouth.

"But the hoof, girl . . . ," he muttered. "Don't you understand? She's lame. The tinker has cheated you— though you are well rid of that cursed coin."

"You can heal her, Grandfather. And I'll do anything to help—whatever you tell me. I'll stay up to soak the hoof night after night. There must be a way."

Grandfather knelt and touched the swell of the ankle and traced the line of the crack. He smelled it and looked deep into the wound. He would be thinking, *a horse to bring back the good days.* Over his bent back and head, the mare and i encouraged each other with every heartbeat.

"We can but try," he said.

We didn't hear Joe returning with Bridey and the milk cart until he had clattered into the yard and called out to us.

"Saints Patrick and Columba! What is it now?" he said. He was quickly out of the cart.

Bridey stretched her neck toward the red mare and nickered.

"Maggie bought her of a tinker," Grandfather began. "The horse was slowing him a bit—you can well see the favor of the hind leg—and he sold her to Maggie cheap. It will be a small job to set her right."

Joe struck his forehead with his palm. "Small job, you say, Grandfather? She's useless. It would be a mercy to put her out of the way. And with what did Maggie buy this beast? She has no secret dowry that I know about."

Bit by bit, the story came out, including the leprechaun and the words that I had taken as a promise.

"Leprechaun, did you say? Maggie has been dealing with the fairy folk? Are you both mad? Maggie, is this true?" Real fear was in his voice.

"Yes, Joe, it is. All of it, though I'm not absolutely sure of the leprechaun for I heard only a voice—but the coin found its way to my hand."

"Had you no thought for the farm, for Grandfather and me? For your own safety?"

"We'll heal the horse, Joe, and she'll win the Galty Prize—the golden guineas will pay the rent and buy us another cow, if you like, to make up for the bullock. It was for you and Grandfather and the farm that I bought the mare. She is a horse with magic in her. She is wise beyond horses."

"Nonsense!" Joe said. "I'll hear no more of this. See that Bridey is fed and watered. She, at least, is of value to us." Joe continued to stare angrily at the mare, as if the whole calamity was her fault, not mine.

But as I went to Bridey, reluctant to leave the mare, I heard my brother sigh. "Grandfather, there's nothing to be done just now except to help this poor animal. We can't let her suffer. Take her to the shed, and I'll get hot water from the house."

"Yes, do that," said Grandfather. "And thank you, Joe. Maggie must have something. This dream means everything to her."

45

I listened with a grateful heart to my grandfather's words, but Joe responded bitterly.

"Let that be the last of the dreams!" he said. "Let me alone with your dreams!"

⊰ CHAPTER 8 ⊱

"A POWERFUL CURE IN THIS BOX"

The mare stood with one hoof in a pail of water hot enough to fog the air in the barn. She munched the fodder that I had set out for her, now and then flicking her tail across her back or turning her head to look at me with questioning eyes. She made no attempt to remove the hoof.

"Are you real? Have you come to save us?" I whispered. "I hardly dare touch you. Will you vanish?" I ran a brush down one foreleg, following with my other hand over the strong tendons, the solid bones.

"Brendan might fear you are worthless. Joe may fear your care will ruin us. Even Grandfather may doubt, but I know you are the queen of horses."

Months of dirt and burrs were caught up in the ragged coat, but under the currycomb it began to come clean and, finally, to gleam. Slowly, the coat became a fit, silky blanket for the mare's elegant frame. It shone, red and gold as autumn. A small white star peeked from beneath her lacy forelock, the only white except for the stocking of the injured leg, hidden inside the pail.

"I've brought you a potato, Maggie."

The words made me look up into Grandfather's face. I realized I hadn't heard him come into the shed and that it wasn't the first time he'd spoken. He stood in the dimming light, holding a lantern and a bowl of potato and milk.

"Oh, Grandfather, she's so beautiful. No finer horse lives in all Ireland. She's ours and real, not a dream anymore." I stood and sipped some of the potato-warm milk from the bowl.

"She's beautiful," Grandfather agreed. "You've made her coat as smooth and soft as the waters of the River Shannon, and it takes lights from the lantern and gives back the glow of rubies. She looks as fine as any horse I ever saw."

"She's beautiful and sturdy, too, and it will be no time before her hoof is as good as new," I said.

"Your words are the strum of a harp to my ears, Maggie, but I fear to expect a miracle."

"Nothing can make me doubt one," I said.

The horse reached her long neck to me and pushed her nose at my ribs, nuzzling, as Bran often did.

I handed the empty bowl to Grandfather and buried my face in the red-gold mane. "Oh, you lovely horse," I said. "You lovely horse. Grandfather, she wants us, too— as much as we wanted her."

"You are both daft," said Joe from the doorway.

Grandfather and I looked to where he stood holding a round tin box with both hands.

"You speak of fairies and horse races while our fine calf is lost to us, and you bring a sick animal to cause worry and eat our hay."

"Joe, I promise—she'll be no loss to you."

"And while you are taking care of her, your potatoes and cabbages will be smothered by weeds and your other jobs forgotten," he said.

"Please, Joe. I won't neglect my chores. I'll work twice as hard to give you more time in your new pasture. The horse won't be a burden, I promise."

"Promises, promises," he muttered. "We'll see about that later. In the meantime I have been to neighbor O'Sullivan's farm to fetch some of that same ointment we used last year when Daisy had the ulcer on her back. There's a powerful cure in this box."

He pushed the tin at me, and I took it with trembling hands. The love I felt for my brother surged in my chest, and I longed to hug him. Instead, I spoke to the horse. "Did you hear that, girl? Joe has brought an ointment to cure your poor hoof. You'll soon be strong and ready to run!"

Later, Grandfather held the lantern high so that the mare and I stood together in its circle of light. "You'll be good for the night, Maggie?"

"Fine, Grandfather, please don't worry. You can leave us." I had strewn the floor with blankets. "We'll be just fine."

The mare, too, assured Grandfather by nickering softly to him from where she stood with the injured hoof bound in hot damp rags.

Across the shed, the cows, Iris and Daisy, were dozing, unconcerned. Old Bridey looked on from a narrow stall, stamped her feet, and swished her tail as

49

Grandfather set down the lantern and left us, closing the cracked and drafty door behind him.

I rubbed the ridge of the mare's mane and scratched under her forelock, unwilling to lie down on the blankets. Even though I was weary, excitement kept me wide-awake. Bran padded to the barn door and cocked his ear toward the cottage, then returned to the stall and picked a blanket of his own to settle on.

Before I finally lay down, I hugged the mare one more time. "Pegasus," I said. "That is your name— Pegasus. You are as noble as the winged horse of the Greek gods, and such a name shows how fast you'll fly."

I pulled gently at Pegasus' ear to be sure the horse heard. "I can call you Peg for short, and that's a good Irish name and rather like my own. Sometimes I'll call you Pegeen, adding the syllable that shows how I love you. Do you like it, Pegasus? Do you like your name?"

The horse blew breath from her nostrils into my hair, making it fly. It was answer enough.

↤ CHAPTER 9 ↦

"DON'T LET THE FEVER TAKE HER DOWN"

By the first rays of dawn filtering into the barn, Pegasus stood under a patchwork of ragged blankets while Grandfather inspected her wound. He traced the line of the crack, smelled the injury and felt above the hoof for tenderness in the pastern.

"Is she better, Grandfather?" I asked, searching his face for encouragement, though the dullness in the mare's eye, the droop to her head, and the angry swell of her ankle told me that Peg's condition was grave.

Grandfather shook his head. "It looks bad, Maggie, very bad. I fear poisoning in her blood."

I touched the pastern gently. The skin beneath the dull hair was hot and puffy.

Grandfather pitched fresh hay into Peg's box. The mare stuck her muzzle into it, blew laboriously through clogged nostrils, and turned away.

I fetched hot water, all the time whispering encouragement to Peg. I washed away the mucus from the mare's eyes and nostrils as the hoof soaked. When the water grew tepid, I applied fresh salve to the wound and sealed the hoof and pastern with mud from the River Tar.

Each time I repeated the treatment, I told myself that the injury was mending. Hadn't such mud closed a deep wound in Grandfather's leg the time he cut himself slicing peat from the bog for us to burn in our hearth? Hadn't it healed burns on a neighbor baby's arm? I looked to Peg, searching for a miracle, but the wise light in her eyes had sunk too far for me to find reassurance.

Grandfather took time from the garden and house to look in and inspect the hoof or bring food, but he said little.

Joe came into the shed only to milk the cows and take them with Bridey to pasture. He didn't ask about Peg, but also he didn't scold me for neglecting my chores. Worry creased his forehead.

By nightfall, I could no longer fool myself. "She's worse, Grandfather," I said, rubbing the mare's shoulder. "See how she stands so listlessly with her bad leg cocked. She won't eat, hardly drinks, and her neck bows lower and lower."

Grandfather nodded and rubbed his hand over Peg's neck and down her shoulder to pat her side. "It's fever from the injury. I hoped she'd be better by now."

I moved closer to Grandfather, and he took my hand.

"The ankle is swollen to at least twice normal size," I said, hoping he'd say I was wrong.

"It must hurt her a great deal."

52

"The swelling will go down by morning. She'll be better. Won't she, Grandfather?"

"Perhaps—I've seen it happen that way."

Fear, as icy as the storm in the Fairy Woods, gripped me. "And sometimes not?"

"And sometimes not."

"She'll be all right, Grandfather. I know she will."

"She's strong." He pursed his lips and squinted at Peg.

"I had a promise in the woods, Grandfather. A horse for a penny. A leprechaun . . . "

"If it was a leprechaun, Maggie, you can be sure he didn't lie, but it's sometimes a puzzle to learn the truth of a fairy promise."

Grandfather knelt in silence to look again at the hoof. Though I couldn't see his face, his worry stirred the air between us like a butter paddle.

For the tenth time that day, I brought hot water from the cottage, bathed the hoof, and again held it in the pail to soak away the infection.

Grandfather stayed with Peg then, while I fetched more water from the well and hung a kettle of it from the crane to heat over the fire. When I returned, Grandfather had applied fresh salve and mud.

"You must keep her on her feet, Maggie, so that her blood moves through her body. Don't let the fever take her down, for some that go down never get up again."

Joe returned with the cows and Bridey late in the afternoon, looking weary. He had been to his new field, clearing it while the animals grazed the field's sparse grass.

"The horse doesn't look much better," Joe said.

"She's worse," I admitted.

"I'll watch her for you while I milk the cows," Joe said, and I went to the cottage to eat. I returned as Joe was storing the milk.

"I'm going out after supper," Joe said. "I'll stop by to see how you're doing when I get back."

"Take care on the road."

"Do I look so dangerous then?"

"After dark, every shadow is a conspirator to Her Majesty's dragoons. It is, after all, against English law for Irish to walk the roads at night." I kissed my hand goodbye to him as he left for the cottage. He'd take his evening meal before setting out to wherever he was going—to Connory Mill, I imagined. I hoped it was to visit Nan Connory and not to conspire with the men.

The lingering springtime sun of Ireland spread the day long past the time when I had eaten supper—potatoes baked in the ashes of the hearth, Grandfather's soda bread, and a tin of milk. The light stayed through hours in which the only changes in Peg's condition were the wheezes and rasps added to her breathing.

When dark finally came, Grandfather brought a lantern and helped me clean and reapply the healing mud and ointment to the hoof.

"Don't give up, girl," he said to Peg, patting her before he left. "Don't give up."

With me beside her in the stall, Peg kept on her feet through the early nighttime hours, shifting her weight and sipping water when I offered it to her. But the breath came hard in the great chest, and I began to despair. "What if she doesn't live?" I said to myself. Even the race and the Cup and the guineas fell back in my mind like upset hurdles as my thoughts raced toward the awful idea that Peg might die.

Sometime before midnight, I dozed and woke to find Peg down on her knees. "Oh, Pegeen." I pulled at Peg's halter. "Please get up. Please try." I pushed my body against the mare's flank to keep her from rolling onto the straw.

Peg's weight bore upon me as if to crush me, but I braced against the wall of the shed and refused to budge. My bones would surely snap and my muscles collapse. The terrible strain chewed at my resolve and strength, while tears ran over my cheeks.

"Don't you know you'll die if you lay yourself in the straw?" I told her. With my fists I beat at her flanks and ribs. "Get up, Peg, get up!" I cried, and Peg's muscles twitched as if she wanted to try, but couldn't.

I pounded and pounded on the downed mare even though each time my fist struck the heaving sides I cried in fear that I was hurting her while trying to help. Finally, seeing I was doing no good, I stopped and laid my head against Peg's shoulder. Through the hours, her hide grew ever more hot with fever, and her breath grew shallow. My own chest constricted, and I understood how breathing had become a great burden to the horse.

"Pegeen, Pegeen, don't die. I've just found you. Don't die." Exhausted though I was from pounding the horse, I got up and pulled forward on Peg's halter, urging and pleading with the mare to get up. When Peg responded by rising to her front knees, I ran around to her tail and pulled on it, trying to get her up behind as well.

Peg began to gather her hind legs under her, but her legs folded and she collapsed again onto her chest.

"I've got to get you up," I said. "I must. Grandfather said you will die if I let you go down." I found a rope in Bridey's empty stall. In desperation, I fashioned a loop for

Peg's rear foot, the uninjured one on which she lay. Frantically, I struggled to tug the rope beneath her body. If I could loop the rope around the hoof and run it under Peg's side, I could pull her to her feet. But I couldn't slip the rope under the hindquarters. Her weight was too much for me to budge.

Time had become a thick river. Through it, I swam in my efforts to help Peg. Somewhere out of that river, Joe's hands gripped my shoulders and pulled me away from the rope. "Easy, Maggie. What you're trying to do will work, but you can't do it alone."

I dropped to the straw-strewn ground, grateful for my brother's return.

"Wait," he told me and was soon back with Grandfather.

Joe put me at Peg's tail to twist and pull upward. He put his own greater strength to the rope at her head. As the two of us tugged, Peg once more tried to help herself. Grandfather was able to pull the rope attached to the ankle. Suddenly, in one great lunge, she was on her feet.

Sweat poured from her as she stood, darkening Joe's shirt and running over my arms.

"Is she dying?"

"No, girl," Joe said. I think the fever is leaving her. All you have done for her is taking effect. Change her blankets, and we'll see if she'll take feed." As he spoke, he pitched hay under the mare's nose.

I pulled the wet blankets from Peg's back, and the mare, standing firm on all four legs, shook herself and nuzzled her head into the hay to eat. For the first time in days, her ears pricked forward, a sure sign she was mending. *I'm back. It's all right.*

Just as the fairy storm had broken and curled into the sky, my fears cracked and let light and gladness back into my mind. On the old blankets in the barn, I sank down at last to sleep. I dreamed of Peg, whole and running over green pastures and down tree-lined roads.

⊰ CHAPTER 10 ⊱

"SHE'LL BE A FLYER"

With that terrible night in the barn in the past, Peg's healing was rapid. The swelling was down in her ankle, and, with another week of soaks and mudpacks, Grandfather pronounced the sickness gone. Through March and April, the hoof grew out and each month strengthened. Brendan Connory brought around the farrier to trim away the last of the cracked hoof and fit Peg with iron shoes.

Peg stamped her left foot, then again, a greeting for me, especially for me. *I am in high spirits today*, she was saying. I held out my hand and Peg licked it, then nuzzled her nose to my palm. She was better, she would run faster than the wind, she was telling me. She was telling everything, all about the time with the Gypsies, how she hurt her foot. I knew everything about Peg. I knew it all.

By May, Grandfather was schooling Peg at the end of a long lead rope, and, under the glaze of an unusually warm sun, I watched the horse, strong and sound after weeks of patience and care. Peg trotted, ears pricked toward Grandfather's voice, her tail held high. Her hooves struck sure on the path, and I swelled with pride and love. Grandfather looked as I had never seen him, almost young, standing in the center of that paddock where he schooled so many horses before I was born. Before the famine took the good times away.

"She'll be a flyer, Maggie. She'll take every wall and tree stump that the Galty course can throw at her."

"Can you be so sure, Grandfather?"

"Aren't you?"

"Oh, yes. I've known since I first saw her."

"Well, now I know, too."

My heart swelled as much at Grandfather's happiness as at Peg's performance in the paddock.

"Then you both know something the saints themselves do not," Joe said. He had joined me to watch Grandfather and Pegasus.

"Joe, even you must see that she's special."

Peg stamped her feet and whinnied.

"Oh, I see that all right."

"Joe, your tone of voice mocks your words, but don't you see what the mare has done for Grandfather?"

"Yes, it has given him something to replace planting cabbages and mending socks, which is the true work needed in this place."

I smiled broadly, not allowing Joe's words and tone to try me. "It's not true. No chore goes undone."

"Now, that'd be a miracle greater than any cure of a broken hoof!"

"But the hoof is cured, Joe. You yourself have witnessed the improvement over these months."

"It's still cracked. It could break again."

"No. We'll take great care until the hoof is grown completely back. Grandfather is sure Peg'll be ready by November."

"So you still think a horse can move the clock back for Shannon Farm?"

"Oh, yes, Joe. You'll see. Pegasus will win the cup and the guineas."

"And that will make a difference, do you think?"

"How could it not?"

Joe shook his head. "Well, I haven't the time to get mixed up in your dreams. The cows must be milked regardless of horse races and trophies."

"Brendan says that Patrick is home. Will you be going to the mill tonight?" Success with Pegasus was making me bold, even with Joe.

"Who said anything about the mill?"

"Is it Nan Connory you go to sneak a look at?"

Joe reddened so that I knew it was at least partly true. He said, "No, not for that. Mind you she's worth the looking, but who would I be to court the daughter of a mill owner?"

"Shannons are just as good!" I shot back.

"Oh—haven't we the temper!"

"It's true. Grandfather is the best horseman in all Tipperary. And our father was a good friend of Mr. Fergus O'Hanlon, a steward at the race, and of Mr. Connory, too. We no longer have our land, but Grandfather says we are as good as the gentry!"

Joe laughed. "Well, anyway, it isn't Nan Connory who takes me to the mill. I go to hear some of what Patrick has to say. He's been to Cork, you know, and even

60

to Dublin. Where else can I hear of things like land reform and ridding Ireland of the union with England."

"Revolution!"

"No, not revolution. The Fenians took that notion down with them to defeat. Do you think I'd mix myself in with them to bring greater ruin on us than was caused by your cows getting into Drummond fields?" He had not mentioned my disgrace for some time, and his next words softened the last, by bringing me further into his confidence. "As it happens, it's mere interest in what's going on in the English parliament and such that takes me to gatherings at the mill. There's some support for home rule even in the Great Halls of England."

The notion filled me with a feeling that I hadn't a name for. My teacher was English, and he allowed no mention of home rule in the classroom. I half expected him to appear in the yard with a cane to rap Joe's knuckles.

"Grandfather doesn't believe The Queen of England and her parliament could ever be made to return an Irish government to Irish soil or allow easier ways for us to regain our lands," I said.

"The time will come. Promises cannot always be broken."

"I can't bother with talk like that," I said. "Shannon Farm is all I care for, and I'll use Peg to get money to buy it for us." That's what I said, but Joe's words troubled me. He might say he wasn't involved in revolution, but wouldn't that depend on how the British Magistrate construed the word? I might be innocent of ideas like "home rule," but I knew that we were always at the mercy of foreign justice.

Grandfather had finished trotting Peg and was now walking at her shoulder, leading her around the path to cool her down. He spoke gently into her ear. I caught only a word or two of Gaelic, the true Irish language that was like a foreign tongue to me.

As he left the ring and came to Joe and me, Grandfather said, "It's been years since I've schooled any horse, Maggie, but as soon as Peg began to move, I felt the blood stir within me, and I thought to see your father run from the stables to help. It was always a special time for him—training a new horse." He sighed. "Well, the stables are gone, but the horse . . . well, it's sure to be a winner."

By the end of June, the path around the paddock was well worn. The sun shone full strength on my back as Peg trotted in the familiar circle at the end of Grandfather's lungeline.

Once again Joe and I watched together from the paddock gate.

"Show Joe how she canters, Grandfather," I said.

Grandfather urged Peg, and the three of us watched as the mare sprang from a walk to the faster pace. She moved gracefully, her tail streaming as she circled the paddock.

"She does look good, Grandfather," Joe said. "Who would have thought the hoof would heal and be so strong?"

"Maggie for one."

Joe looked at the horse again, his eyes, for once, a little dreamy, too. "Perhaps tomorrow," he said, "we can put a saddle on her."

The mare, still circling the paddock, caught my eye with her own. Promises flew between us.

⊰ CHAPTER 11 ⊱

A SPECIAL GIFT

I was up with cockcrow the next morning. I had chores to do and had promised to stop by the mill before noon to visit Brendan's mother. Late in the afternoon, when the cows were safe in the barn, I would saddle Pegasus and ride!

Sitting beside Grandfather, I gulped my porridge while he sipped tea and smoked.

"Wolfing your breakfast won't swallow the hours between now and the time to ride, Maggie." Grandfather's eyes sparkled.

"I can't help it, Grandfather. I can hardly wait."

"I think Peg is excited, too," Grandfather said. "She was calling from the shed."

"She's just hungry and ready for pasture," said Joe, coming through the door from the barn. "Will you be along soon, Grandfather? The cows are milked and ready."

"If you want me to, Grandfather," I interrupted, "I could go to pasture for you while Joe delivers the milk to the Big House. I can visit the mill another time."

"I've been taking cows to pasture since I was far younger than you, Maggie. I look forward to the times when both you and Joe have other duties and leave me the cows. You run on to the mill. Mrs. Connory has something for you, I think."

I tied potatoes and soda bread in two separate handkerchiefs and hurried them, along with water jugs, to Joe and Grandfather. Joe stood beside Bridey and the rickety four-wheeled cart carrying our three large jugs of milk. The day was soft, gentle moisture beading on our faces. Bridey wouldn't need a hat to shield her eyes from the sun.

Coming out of the barn, Peg saw me and whinnied. She was asking, *Will you be coming with me?* Or maybe, *What adventure have you planned for us?*

I left my place at Bridey's head and ran to Peg. "You're going with Grandfather; don't you see," I told the mare, scrubbing my knuckles against Peg's nose. "Good sweet grass for you . . . Then we'll see. Then we'll see."

Peg pawed the ground with one forefoot, then the other.

Joe tapped Bridey with a stick, and the old horse ambled out of the yard with Joe and me walking one on either side as the cart clattered up the road toward the mill and Drummond's.

Grandfather, the cows, and Peg walked down the road to pasture. Peg danced sideways to keep me in view, and I waved her on her way until we lost each other around a bend in the road.

"Have you ever been inside the Big House, Joe?" I asked over Bridey's neck as we walked.

"There's an office in the barn for the business I have at Drummond House."

"Grandfather has been inside many times. The winners of the Galty Race were always asked to tea."

"In the old days, Maggie."

"Grandfather says there's a lamp hung with crystals like diamonds and blazing with a hundred candles. He says . . ."

"What is needed with a hundred candles?"

"And he says they have a piano, grander than the one Nan Connory has at the mill."

"A piano is nice all right," Joe agreed, "though I much prefer the softness of the harp. And the bagpipes are good for getting the feet to move."

I jumped to get a better look at my brother over Bridey's back. Yes, he seemed happy. Oh, I was glad to catch him feeling that way.

"I wonder how many rooms are in the Big House, Joe? A thousand, do you think? I've heard they sometimes invite a hundred people to hunt, and sleep them all afterward."

"Maybe."

"I'm glad we don't have to care for such a house and feed the servants and all. I much prefer our cottage, poor as it is, but . . ."

"But you wouldn't mind peeking inside the Big House just once."

"That's not what I was going to say at all. I was just going to say that I long for the day when we can own our cottage and pastures."

"You'll be leaving one day, Maggie, to go to another cottage, and Grandfather—well, Grandfather is old. Perhaps it's not so important after all."

"Not important, Joe? Not important! It is the most important thing of all. Grandfather isn't old. Someday, maybe you'll want a wife. There will be room for us all."

"Some give up and cross the great ocean to America, Maggie."

"Not us. We'll never emigrate! Remember when the three Greaney boys went? A proper wake was held before they sailed and more wailing and crying from the ones left behind than if the boys had truly died. I will never leave Ireland."

"Still the Greaney boys send back coin from time to time, more than we'll ever have."

"That's not true, Joe! You'll see. We'll have coins aplenty after Peg races."

Yet, the sunny feeling, while chattering to Joe about the Big House, had been edged out. I remembered the Finnertys, driven from their acres and living under an overturned wagon. But, no, I pushed the picture from my mind. Peg would save us.

"Don't ever think of giving up!" I said.

"Well, that's still to be seen," Joe said. "For now, we have reached the road to the mill. Get on with you. Don't forget to be home before dark."

"Joe—you know I'll be there at milking time."

"Oh, yes, the saddling of the mare. It had skipped from my mind."

Of course he had not forgotten, I knew. It had been an opportunity for him to tease me. But I smiled and waved goodbye, running up the road so as not to be late.

Mrs. Connory sat me at her kitchen table, setting a blue mug of steaming tea and a pitcher of cream before me. On the table was a plate of sandwiches, too, some with jam and some with potted meat, and sweet cakes besides. I tasted the blend of flavors in the tea while I felt the softness of the rag rug under my curled toes and enjoyed the scent of summer flowers, bending from a china bowl on the table. Shiny pewter and bright platters lined the dressers. I would never tire of this room, and Connory House had other fine rooms, some beyond a staircase of polished wood.

"Brendan tells us that you have a horse now, Margaret Kathleen," Mrs. Connory said, seating herself across from me and pouring cream into her own mug of tea. It was just the two of us, Nan being in town with her father for the day.

"A brave mare, ma'am," I said. "Her name is Pegasus. We'll have her ready for the Galty."

"Like the old days for your grandfather. I remember what a fine horseman he was. And your father, too. What a handsome man on a horse!"

"And was my mother pretty, Mrs. Connory?"

"Oh, yes, Maggie. She looked like you when she was your age, though her hair was pure red, not mixed, the way yours is, with that fine brown color of the Shannon men." She studied me for a moment. "And her eyes were green as yours, the exact shade—I was in Kerry once and the sea there is no greener."

The two of us sat in silence for a while. I imagined both my mother's eyes and the green sea of Kerry while Mrs. Connory concentrated on the pattern for the shirt. I had never been to Kerry and I didn't remember my mother.

In the way of thoughts, mine came round to another question. "Mrs. Connory, what do the men talk about when they gather at the mill of an evening? Joe is ever visiting here when Patrick is home. He returns to us with new thoughts. I asked Brendan, but he told me only a little. Do they talk politics?"

"A little, I imagine, but mostly cows and crops." Mrs. Connory continued to cut with her long black shears. "And much about horse races and hurling games."

I understood that I wasn't to learn more of what talk went round at the mill so far as she was concerned.

Then Mrs. Connory got up and went to the dresser. "Which reminds me, it will soon be your birthday— fourteen you'll be in August. Isn't that right?" She brought a package from the dresser.

"Yes, that's right."

"Well, this is something I fixed for you from an old skirt of mine. Not much of a present, but something I thought you'd need. Do you mind that it's early?

I smiled as Mrs. Connory handed me the folded skirt. It was brown as autumn leaves. I shook it out and found it was cut and seamed at the middle so that the sides were divided, like wide pantaloons.

"It would be a scandal in some parts to wear a skirt so much like a man's trousers, I suppose, but I saw a lady in Dublin who wore one like it to ride. She was an eccentric—that means she had a mind of her own, Maggie, not dictated to by others' wills. She said that sitting astride a horse was the only safe and sensible way."

I sat speechless, staring at the skirt. I had been allowed to tuck up my skirts and ride Bridey around the yard and pastures, but now I saw how impossible it would be for me to do that at the Galty meet. Fine ladies rode sidesaddle, their skirts sweeping over their ankles and feet, even at hunts. But I would never keep my seat on a sidesaddle over the wild Galty course. In all my dreams and plans, I had never thought of this before then.

I didn't know how I arrived in Mrs. Connory's arms, but there I was, hugged and giving thanks through a blur of tears, while her gentle voice went on. "Your grandfather was here after a saddle for you last week. It wasn't begged, you understand, it was payment of a debt—some rye brought in to the mill last year, I believe—and I knew right away it would be for you. It was a man's saddle, but men never think of such things as how a girl can sit in a man's saddle with an ordinary skirt."

"Mrs. Connory, my own mother couldn't be—"

"Hush, Maggie, your own mother was an angel. And we all miss her. You are too young to remember, too young when she was taken by fever, but I can tell you no one was finer." Mrs. Connory looked dreamy for a moment then said, "Try it on, Maggie, and then we'll see how you like my bread and jam."

When we finished tea, I sat down to help Mrs. Connory with some sewing, the new skirt feeling soft against my legs.

Mrs. Connory gave me a piece of linen and thread to stitch a shirt for Joe, and though my fingers were stiff and clumsy, Mrs. Connory taught me with patience. We bent together over the cloth until the door opened and both Connory boys burst in, followed by the Connory dogs. The room filled with boots and laughter, hats flung aside, dog and gun smells, and boundless energy.

"Rabbits for Madam Connory," Brendan said, sweeping a grand bow to his mother and plopping the poor dead things onto her table. I jumped from my stool.

Patrick caught me as I ran to fetch a tray to put the rabbits on. He whirled me to the middle of the floor. "And what have we here?" he said. "A visiting duchess? One of Queen Vic's girls, no doubt?" I felt conscious of my bare feet even with the new skirt. Patrick Connory! With his arms around me!

Mrs. Connory pulled her son away. "Hush, Patrick, it's Maggie Shannon come to visit, and she'll think you've been drinking pocheen rather than hunting rabbits! She's a young lady, now, not the baby you used to tease."

It became my turn for bows, from Patrick and Brendan both. "Oh, a young lady, is it?" said Brendan. "And where then is the hoyden who is to beat the lads in the Galty chase?"

I was caught between delight and panic at the boisterous behavior. I had known the Connory boys all my life. Patrick was a wilder version of my brother Joe, the two of them so much older that they were nearly objects of worship. Brendan, only two years older than I was, had been my protector, playmate, and more recently, my conspirator at the Gypsy camp. Now he was teasing and wildly brash. Where did I stand with him?

The confusion lasted for only a moment before Brendan spun me out the door to where his Sultan and Patrick's Cashel waited for the ride to Shannon Farm.

"Am I really to ride Sultan?" I asked.

"Since Patrick has given me Cashel for the afternoon, I don't see why not."

He bent over me, holding Sultan's bridle and steadied the stirrup as I set my foot and hoisted myself onto the horse's back, my new skirt perfectly accommodating itself to Brendan's saddle. He smiled up at me as he handed me the reins. While I had been indoors with Mrs. Connory, the sun had come out and was now warming my back and the air that stirred between his face and mine.

⊰ CHAPTER 12 ⊱

SADDLE AND RIDE

Back on Shannon Farm once more, I took Peg's reins and swung onto the mare's back for the first time, letting my skirt ride above my knees on either side. The special skirt from Mrs. Connory would wait for race day. I had changed to my regular clothes and put away the gift as soon as I got home.

A great energy flowed from Peg to me, as if we shared one heart to push the blood through our legs and bodies and one mind for the dream that filled us both, the dream of winning.

"It's my feeling," Grandfather said as he adjusted the saddle's cinch, "that she's a natural jumper. Just look at the deep chest and strength of the back legs. It is you, Margaret Kathleen Shannon, who will be taught!" Grandfather's eyes, pale as glass, twinkled with vitality as he spoke.

I smiled down at him, feeling my own happiness radiate toward Grandfather. "Yes, Grandfather, I'm sure you're correct, but I hope I'm quicker at my studies in the paddock than in the schoolhouse."

"If you're as quick, you will be expert before another phase of the moon." He placed his hands over mine. "Hold the reins just so," he told me, adjusting my fingers on the leather straps. "You can be ever so gentle with her mouth. She'll respond to the least pressure of your legs."

I moved Peg into a high-stepping walk that was nearly a prance, around the paddock and back and forth. Every cell of my body felt the rhythm of Peg's gait. It was all coming true! Peg was well and strong, and the day I had looked forward to all spring and summer, the day I could ride, was here at last.

"See how glad she is, Grandfather," I said. "She feels what I feel, and, see, she turns almost before I can command her. She knows what I want at the instant I know. She is everything we've wanted."

"You might speak too soon, girl. She bears your weight well enough, but you haven't trotted her, much less run her. You haven't taken her over the hurdles. You mustn't polish that cup before it rests on our fireplace mantle." Whatever his words, Grandfather had set his eyes fast on Peg, and jubilation tugged the corners of his mouth.

And so, we continued through summer. Grandfather watched for any sign of faltering as I trotted Peg, cantered her, and finally pushed her to a full-out run. But Peg was strong and able, carrying me with ease and responding to commands quickly and surely. What Grandfather had said proved true—Peg was the teacher and I the pupil.

Late in August, shortly after my fourteenth birthday, I began to take Peg onto the road for gallops and down to Connory's to try her in what Grandfather had named "the schooling field." The field had been a woodlot. Connorys had begun to clear it for planting, but somehow the work had not gone beyond felling the trees and hauling some away.

"It's just what we want for Peg," I told Grandfather. "The logs lying all crisscross and helter-skelter are just the thing to strengthen legs and teach Peg to be sure-footed."

"The very thing!" Grandfather said. "I should have thought of it myself."

First under Grandfather's scrutiny and later alone, I rode Peg in the field, guiding the mare so that she must find her way between and over the jumble of fallen trees. I felt as though I sat on a rocking horse as Peg's body rose and fell over the barriers.

I thrilled to see how quickly Peg learned to pick up her feet and make her way through the maze without grazing a single log with her hooves. Each time we finished, Peg would turn her head and prick her ears, looking and listening for the praise that was always in my eyes and on my tongue.

After little more than a week of the strenuous exercises in the field, Brendan helped me raise some of the logs to make ever-higher hurdles, though he complained that it was of no use for a Gypsy nag who hadn't a chance against his Sultan, less so against Patrick's Cashel. Still, as he grumbled, he had a smile in his eyes.

Peg took the hurdles from a trot and, finally, in the last warm days of summer, from a canter, clearing each log with inches to spare.

74

"Remember, Maggie, your main job with Peg will be just to stay on her back and not interfere with her balance and stride," Grandfather said. "Peg loves the jumps. Her eye is quick to see what she must do, and her legs quick to follow. Lean forward with your hands well up on her neck and go with her. You'll see some riders lean away from the jumps, but that can unbalance a horse."

I learned well. Peg's steadiness and sure feet helped me keep my seat so that I seldom felt myself slip going over the jumps. I looked forward to the day when Grandfather and I would take her over the Galty course itself. "A rough track," he had said, "through woods and into bogs with barriers thrown up as nature and the fence builders planned them, not set about all neat and tidy in an open field."

But the race was still far off in November, and, after harvest, I returned to school. Many of my classmates had left off studies to help with grown-up tasks, but Grandfather had insisted that I keep up my lessons. "The English schoolmasters are not so keen as those we had in the hedgerows when we squatted outdoors to learn in all weather," Grandfather would tell me. "Still, this one knows his Greek and Latin, and you should return."

I rode Peg to school, Brendan and Sultan joining us at the mill. I was in my next to last year, and Brendan went twice a week to help the schoolmaster, sometimes more often if he wasn't needed at home.

On our way we passed knots of barefoot children, each with a sack holding a noon potato and such penny books as he or she owned. They walked in family groups, the bigger children carrying peat logs for the schoolhouse fire.

"I feel almost too grand," I said, "riding Peg while others walk."

"You are grand, Maggie. Others will not so much envy you as enjoy the sight of you and your fine horse."

"That's just blab, Brendan." I looked at him shyly from the corner of my eye.

"I rather enjoy the sight of you myself."

I could not look at Brendan after he said that. "Have you been to Blarney Castle, then, Brendan, to kiss the famous stone and learn flattery?" I asked him, pretending to smooth a tangle from Peg's well-combed mane.

"My brother, Patrick, has—me holding his legs so he could swing out to it from the top stones of the castle. Does that count?"

"Race?" I asked for want of what to say next. I was not so good at teasing as was Brendan.

Peg's hooves pounded out the rhythm of the gallop, while I envisioned and felt the day of the Galty race as sharply as I felt the sun on my back. Beside us, Sultan matched Pegasus stride for stride and Brendan looked born to the saddle. They had raced last year, second only to Patrick and Cashel. Who was I to think that I could match him with only a few months' practice and a Gypsy's horse?

⊰ CHAPTER 13 ⊱

"MAGGIE SHANNON ON THE TINKER'S HORSE!"

The stewards resisted my entry at first. Many fine ladies rode in Irish hunts, but this was a cross-country race, not a hunt, and I was not Lady Shannon, only Maggie.

"I stood firm before them, Maggie," Grandfather told me when he came out of the meeting with the racing board. "They remember me, Thomas Shannon, and my horse, Seaneen. They remember your father." He stood tall and proud.

"I knew they wouldn't refuse," I said, though I had bitten my nails and sat twisting my hair while I waited outside that meeting room. I was dressed as I would dress on race day.

"Come on home now, while I tell you the rest," Grandfather said.

Mounted on Peg and Bridey, we rode like gentry, Grandfather in his best coat and britches, I with the wonder of boots on my feet, Mrs. Connory's skirt, and a fine russet jacket to match.

The jacket and boots had been my father's when he had been a lad and only a bit too large for me. Nothing new had come into our house in twenty years, but the boots and jacket of the young Garrett Shannon had been preserved in Grandfather's storeroom for this very day.

"I rang my guinea on the table with such force that one of the stewards had to clap his hand over the coin to stop its wild spinning. 'Who in this room has won the Galty twice, other than I, Thomas Shannon?' I demanded. 'Do you dare deny me?'"

"The same guinea you took from the wall to show me?"

"The very same. Just as we must save one from this year's purse."

"You're still sure we'll win; aren't you, Grandfather?"

"And you, Maggie?"

"Just as sure." Though I put bravery in my mouth, my heart beat unsurely. So much depended on me, and I had never won any prize greater than a second-place at spelling.

The day of my dreams and fears came at last. The day, that had lived in my mind on gallops with Brendan, the day that I'd prepared for endlessly on the schooling field, now dazzled me with sunshine. Soft rain had fallen overnight, and at Drummond House, small puddles winked from leaf cups. Weathered walls shone like green jewels. The sky and all the world wished us well. I was sure of it.

"They are all here for you," I whispered to Peg. "They've come to see the best horse in all of Ireland win the Galty Chase." I patted my words into Peg's shoulder

78

and felt the delicious shivering of Peg's flesh beneath the glossy hide. I looked for Grandfather and found him standing proudly, his coat brushed and buttoned, a scarf at his throat. He tipped his hat and winked. I guided Peg to where he stood. I looked for Joe in the crowd, but didn't expect to find him. He'd said he hadn't time for horse races and foolishness. But I couldn't help hoping. If Joe had come, I would have taken it as a sign more powerful than the sun shining on my face.

"You look very like your father, Maggie," Grandfather said. "And you are as smart in the saddle."

"Thank you, fine sir," I teased. "But it's Peg and her trainer, my illustrious grandfather, you should be watching, not me."

"Go on now, and win!"

As the other riders did, I moved Peg back and forth over every inch of the great yard, with Peg swishing her tail and my heart drumming. Grand ladies watched from the porch of the Big House while the riders paraded. Pipes squawked, and scrubbed children from the cottages pranced and slapped their thighs, their small fists holding make-believe reins. They were mount and rider both, tossing their heads and whinnying. I had been like them not many years before, barefoot and full of dreams.

The horses and riders were blurs of bright hunt coats and gleaming hides as I guided Peg through their midst. Now and then a familiar face separated itself from the brilliant scene. The steward of the race, Mr. Fergus O'Hanlon, who had been my father's friend, sat straight and tall on his big roan. His black jacket shone like ebony over the dappled red of his horse. His burnished boots gleamed in the sun. And, of course, I was always aware of Patrick on black Cashel and Brendan Connory on bay Sultan whenever they appeared now and then among the other riders.

Patrick's coat was bold emerald, and he wore an emerald scarf at his throat. The green was a statement of his belief that Ireland should separate from England, Brendan had told me. Brendan's coat was chestnut brown, but he had woven green into Sultan's mane. I was sure the English magistrate and Sir Henry Fitzhenry Drummond had taken note, though they would hesitate to bring charges against young men of the Connory family, certainly not on race day in Tipperary.

Peg snorted and whistled for the attention of Sultan, whom she knew well.

"Won't Sultan think you're a flirt, girl?" I told Peg. I wanted to go where Brendan was, but I was conscious of the many eyes and felt shy.

Breezing Peg outside the track, giving her a slow canter to warm her blood for the race, I lived through the final moments before the race riding in a dream. The warmth of the other riders enveloped me. I was a girl among young men and grown men, but they treated me as one of them. I gloried in the admiring glances directed toward Peg.

Brendan and Sultan passed close, and Brendan whispered, "I wish you well, Maggie. You may have got your mare from a tinker, but she's a beauty." I felt my cheeks redden with pleasure.

My friend moved into place beside me at the end of a row of fifteen other horses and riders. A hush settled over the crowd. Peg's ears flicked forward as the starter, standing to one side and several yards in front of us all, raised a flag in his right hand. A great gold watch gleamed in his left. The riders started walking their horses forward, keeping them nose to nose. As they approached him, the starter called out, "Ready!"

I sucked in my breath, and, before I could expel it, the flag flashed down and the riders shouted. I pushed Pegasus into a gallop toward the far pasture fence, my heart racing faster than the hooves that pounded on every side.

Grandfather's words, "Hold on and let Peg find her way," thrummed in my head. I gripped tightly with my legs and rose above Peg's withers, leaning over the great neck, my hands holding the reins and also tangled in Peg's mane. Peg took off, and we soared over the first fence with horses on either side. Flying manes and coattails flicked by. In my ears, the sounds of creaking leather and hard-breathing horses.

Could I keep my seat for the long race that lay ahead? Hardly checking her pace, Peg scrambled with the others down the steep bank to the road, skidding and sliding. I clung to Peg's mane and looked for holes in the pack that boxed us in. When I had taken Peg over the course with Grandfather riding alongside on Bridey, I had not imagined the crush of flying horses and the noise of so many hooves.

At the bottom of the bank, a low stone wall was hardly there as Peg flew it and galloped down the road. The road would have eventually taken us to the town of Cahir if that had been where we were headed. Its surface was hard, but without dust because of the rain. It gave up a sharp, earth smell that mingled with the scent of harness oils and the pungent odors of perspiration. Peg's breath came steady and strong, unlabored and confident.

A curve in the road put the knot of horses at bristly hedgerows of gorse. The horses sailed, twos and threes, Peg among them, over the spiky gorse toward

81

Drummond's woods. I found a break in the pack and slipped Peg through. Free of the crush, the mare lengthened her stride. I saw clearly that the leaders were Patrick on Cashel and a white jumper ridden by a man in a red coat. At my knee flashed Sultan's nose.

Brendan called, "Ho, Maggie, ride!" He pushed Sultan even with Peg. "Shortcut. Follow me. Don't be afraid. It's allowed."

Peg and I followed Brendan through brush and brambles to the side of the path and plunged with him down a bank with a treacherous ditch at the bottom.

"Look sharp!" he called.

Peg paced Sultan without a falter as they lunged from the ditch onto the flat just before the dangerous barriers of Old Tree Stumps. Now Brendan and I were in front of the red coat and the white horse. Only Cashel led us.

We pounded toward the jagged teeth of Old Tree Stumps, uneven rows of stumps hedged by a rock fence that loomed to the left as Peg sailed the stumps.

Patrick shouted energetically in a hound's voice, and I saw him fling an arm into the air as he and Cashel landed just ahead of us. I felt my breath leave me. I praised God as it returned when Peg's feet touched ground and galloped on.

"See you back at the Big House," Brendan shouted to me, nosing Sultan ahead as we drove toward a second row of stumps and logs.

You'll see Peg's heels before you see the Big House, I thought. A great clatter of the following horses and the calling of their riders filled the silence as Peg's hooves lifted in flight over the stumps.

"Peg, that was brave! Brave girl! Brave girl!" I said as Peg's feet struck earth on the other side. First the left front, then the right only seconds later. The rear feet landed together making the sound of a single *callop* with those of Sultan . . . but then Sultan stumbled and lost a step to Peg, who surged ahead.

Shouts behind told that a horse had gone down over the stumps as we three leaders, Patrick, Brendan and I, moved in an arc to strike the path between a stand of pine and a low stone wall. I gave Peg her head to take the path, flying the wall and then quickly two more, all this as we dizzily galloped down a rough hillside.

Cashel's hindquarters rose and fell beyond Peg's shoulder, and, on the mare's other side, Sultan held steady, only a nose behind. "Fly, girl, fly," I urged, and Peg stretched out and began to move up on Cashel. Sultan fell back. Then Peg and Cashel rose as one horse over a third wall.

I felt the powerful bunch of Peg's muscles beneath me. The mare's lathered sweat soaked my legs and hands.

Peg landed and struck out for the final hurdle of the set. Beside her, Cashel landed poorly, and I saw Patrick unable to ready him for the next wall. He would need to wheel and go at the wall again. Pegasus, meanwhile, cleared the last wall without a missed step. She then navigated the rocks and ridges of the hillside as if they weren't there. Nearly to Devil's Bog, I heard the shouts of Brendan, Patrick, and the others fade behind.

"Go easy, Peg," I whispered. "Don't slip."

The words were all the warning Peg needed to slide from downhill gallop into a high-stepping pace that saw us through the spongy peat. The bog, that could snap the leg of an unwary animal, sucked at Peg's hooves. At one bog hole the mare sank nearly to her chest, and my boot brushed the peat. But Peg surged free and struggled out of the muck onto fair ground. Every step was a step further ahead of the pack.

No sooner were we on hard road than we came to a series of logs. Trees had been felled especially for the race—not high barriers, but trunks placed dangerously close together.

"It's just like the logs at Connory's woodlot, Peg," I encouraged, shutting my eyes and letting Peg have her head, depending on the uncanny ability of the mare to make her way.

Shouts of alarm and whoops of glee swirled behind us, thrilling me. Ahead, watchers lined the road on either side.

"Here's Maggie Shannon on the tinker's horse!" they shouted.

And then, "Maggie Shannon, Maggie Shannon! Ride, Maggie, ride!" I didn't know so many knew my name.

I let Peg go, let her fly down the road. Sultan or Cashel would need impossible strides to catch her. Flecks of foam wetted my arms. The red-gold mane of the mare blew over my face and stung my cheek. I shook my head and, like Peg's mane, my hair came loose and streamed behind me.

Ahead rose the hill we must climb to the finish. Incredibly, I could hear no other hoofbeats as Peg left the road. She began the gallop up the hill, alone among the sixteen that started. At the top of the hill was a stone wall I knew hid a ditch of water. Peg would remember it, too.

We cleared the wall at the top of the hill and carried over to the far side. Peg's heels made a splash at the very edge of the ditch before she began the last run to the pasture gate.

The gate was the last hurdle and Peg took it easily. The finish line, hung with tiny flags, gave before Peg's chest. She carried it with her another couple of yards before it fell beneath her hooves.

We did it! sang my heart, sang Peg's.

As Peg slowed, I sagged forward in the saddle, circling the mare's grand neck with my arms. The mare responded by whinnying and snorting a kind of victory cry.

I brought Peg to a walk, cooling her down as we rode toward the paddock.

Along our way, gentry and common people alike cheered and crowded toward us. Hands on either side reached for Peg's wet flanks and patted her rippling shoulders. They reached to touch me, too. Friends and neighbors told me of their pleasure and pride in me.

"Never has there been so brave a rider, never so strong a horse."

The other riders now had brought their mounts over the last hurdles and added to the crush in the paddock. A garland of pungent leaves was lifted over Peg's head, and Grandfather stepped up proudly to take the reins and lead us to the judges.

"Not a missed step, Grandfather. It's like a miracle."

The silver cup, heavy with guineas, filled my two hands as the victory filled my heart. I slid from Peg's back and walked with Grandfather, to thank Sir Henry Drummond and the other stewards of the race. Beside me, Peg pranced like the great hero she was.

"It's a miracle, Grandfather," I said again.

"Like magic, Maggie." Tears streaked his leathery cheeks.

Into my mind came the years of dreaming, then the schemes and the digging, the terror of the woods and the months of caring for Peg and training her. All had drained through the funnel of the race. Only a residue was left, a small pebble of fear lodged against my ribs. Grandfather had warned of a leprechaun's gift.

⊰ CHAPTER 14 ⊱

A HEAVY BAG OF GOLD

When Joe returned home, at least an hour after Grandfather and I had fed and stabled the horses, his eyes went first to the mantle where the Galty trophy awaited his gaze.

"You did it!" Emotion clotted his voice as he turned toward me. "You did it, Maggie. I was wrong to disbelieve."

I rushed into his arms and felt the rare experience of his embrace, smelled the good masculine odors of warm damp wool, soil and hay. His coat scratched my cheek and nearly suffocated me, so hard did he clasp me.

Finally, he held me at arm's length, as if he must see that I was really his sister and not a changeling spirit.

"It's Peg you must thank, Joe," I said. "She did it herself. All I needed was pray that I didn't fall off over the jumps."

"And the gold," Grandfather said, handing Joe the small pouch of coins. "Heft these. They have the weight of changes for Shannon Farm."

Joe took the bag from Grandfather's hand. "It's heavy," he said, smiling grandly and raising it high.

"Guineas," Grandfather said. "Like the old days." He gathered both of us, Joe and me, in his arms.

The last time I had approached the gates to the Big House on foot, I had been leading the little bullock, barefoot and in disgrace over the ruin of Drummond's fields. Now I walked at my brother's side with a lift in my heart. Beneath Joe's carefully brushed coat, the pouch of gold coins hung from his belt. He wore Grandfather's felt hat and a shirt with a collar.

We had hardly spoken since the night before when we had stood in awe as the gold spilled over our table. But this morning Joe had hitched the pouch to his belt and motioned me to follow him.

"We must have enough coins to pay the rent this year and for some years more," I said, wondering how money translated into numbers of bullocks, jugs of milk or bushels of rye. "How many do you think?"

"I'm not thinking of rent at all," Joe said, "but the price of the farm itself."

"I wasn't sure. I hoped . . . ," I stammered. "But do you think Drummond will sell?"

"It's Irish land, Maggie. There must be a way to get back what is ours. One day Sir Henry Drummond can go back to England where he belongs!"

We fell silent as we approached the great doors. I was stunned by Joe's outburst.

A man in a long coat and gleaming white shirt greeted us. With a proud lift to his head, he asked us to wait, then returned to usher us inside the house. My boots tapped across the marble tiles of the entry, then over polished wood, and, finally, were silenced by spongy wool rugs. I kept my eyes firmly on Joe's back so that I wouldn't gape at the wonders I glimpsed on every side.

Led into Sir Henry's study, we stood before a shiny burlwood desk topped with butter-colored leather on which stood inkpots of ruby glass.

"You have come with your rents in coin?" Sir Henry asked from his chair behind the desk. "I congratulate you on your good fortune, Shannon. The race was well run."

"I would have you take all the coins and deed us back the farm," Joe answered, his hands clasped to Grandfather's hat.

Sir Henry shook his bearded head and tapped a finger on the desktop. "It isn't enough. Your farm is especially valuable for being near the central fields of my barony."

"The land is only a parcel compared to your great holdings. Shannons owned it free and clear before the Hunger." Joe dared place his palm on the desk. I could hear the thin paring of anger growing beneath the words.

"Since that time," Sir Henry said, "my family has always been fair to yours and to our other tenants." The big man stood, and I could see that he, too, was angry.

"But the land is rightly ours," Joe said. "It was English laws and taxes that took it from us when we were helpless."

"So that's how you think, is it?" Sir Henry said, growing red above his starched collar. "The next thing I know you'll be preaching separation from England like those Fenian devils!" He glowered at us both from behind his desk. "You can settle your rent account with my steward."

89

It was a dismissal, I understood. He would not even consider us. I shrank toward the door.

Joe turned on his heel, nearly trampling me in his haste to leave. Grandfather's hat, which had been in Joe's hands, he now slammed onto his head.

But, before he reached the door, Sir Henry's once-again-calm voice called him back. "Oh, Shannon, I am most impressed by your mare. If you should ever wish to sell her, I would be generous."

My heart gave a small leap, but Joe was quick to answer. "Pegasus is the great pride of my sister and not mine to sell. Good day to you now, sir."

"Ah, well, perhaps another time something can be worked out," Sir Henry said quietly, almost to himself, as Joe pushed me from the room.

He is an enemy, thought I. *He will never leave Ireland. He'll never get Peg, that's for sure.*

"The gold drags at me," Joe said, clutching the pouch through the fabric of his coat as he walked. "It should give me strength, but the weight of it slows my feet."

My stomach recoiled over Joe's torment. A young lifetime of labor had hardened his muscles, and his bones and sinews had withstood accidents aplenty as he had battled the stones of the land. Why should he be made to feel weak and without force?

"It's my land," his voice went on. "It was my ancestors claimed it from forest. It is my hand that sets plow to it each spring, and it's my work that has dragged crops from the ground so that others may profit. Didn't Grandfather and his children starve rather than forego paying rent on cottages that were no better than hovels? On patches of land that were mostly rocks and bog?"

He clenched his fists into weapons. "Maggie, our family is less than sheep, important only as occupants who clutter a landscape that would make a better fox hunt were we not there."

The bitter words beat at my ears. I said, "It will get better." I tried to believe it, for him as much as for myself.

"Drummond will never allow us to own. It's all I have worked for, this land, and now gold will not buy it! The land is the only wealth, and Shannons are paupers!" He wrenched the pouch from his belt and took the coins in his hand. I thought he would fling them from his open palm, but instead he closed his fingers around them so tightly that they must bite his flesh.

"Blast the Queen!" he said. "Blast all monarchs ever! Blast Sir Henry Fitzhenry Drummond with his Irish land and English titles!"

We will see more gold! I wanted to cry to him. *Pegasus will win again and again like Boru's horse and we'll have enough. Sir Henry will not refuse us when we can pay more.* But my tongue had bolted itself to the roof of my mouth, and I couldn't speak. I walked in misery beside my brother and his pain.

⊰ CHAPTER 15 ⊱

SOLDIERS FAR FROM HOME

I pushed the excitement of the race and the disappointment in Drummond's office to the back of my mind. The sweetness of the one made bitter by the memory of the other. School filled the short icy days, and I spent the early evenings in Shannon cottage or, like today, stitching a flannel shirt by the Connory hearth.

"How is your grandfather, Maggie?" Mrs. Connory asked. She stood across the kitchen, using a large wooden spoon to stir the day's soda bread in a brown ceramic bowl large enough to hold a week's potatoes.

"He's keeping well, thank you, though the cold makes him stiff. He'll be warmer because of this shirt."

"You could buy more flannel, Maggie, with some of your prize money. I'd be happy to help you with your patterns and cutting. You know that."

"No. This one bolt will have to do. Most of the coins must be saved in case we can convince Sir Henry to let us buy the farm." I set my work aside for a moment to turn my boots that were drying on the hearth. "Joe says it's made to seem a crime for an Irishman to want a piece of the ground on which God placed him."

"That's true enough," said Mrs. Connory. "Mr. Connory says the laws will never be just for Ireland so long as the only parliament is in England."

I pulled my shawl closer about my shoulders. I had come a step closer to knowing about the conversations of the men when they gathered at the mill.

Mrs. Connory filled a skillet with the bread mixture and set it in the hearth, near the fire, then rubbed her hands before the flames. "I don't know when I've seen such a cold winter," she said. "I hear it snows nearly daily in the north."

"Schoolmaster has asked for two bricks of turf for each day's fire, but many can't bring their share. Some don't come on the coldest days. I'm lucky for my father's boots."

I returned to my stitching, and Mrs. Connory began to put away the kitchen things she'd been using to make the bread. She said, "And how are your studies going, Maggie? Brendan tells me you're a good student."

"Brendan is a great help to Schoolmaster, Mrs. Connory. But I sometimes feel I have three masters— schoolmaster and Brendan by day, with Grandfather by night, ever after me with Irish stories, giving me two Celtic kings for every piece of English history I bring home from school."

"Doesn't he approve of what you are taught by the Crown's teachers?"

"Oh, he approves mightily of the Greek and Latin and the figuring, but he fears we are filled too much with English victories and triumphs. He says there's nothing for Irishmen to rejoice in Wellington crushing Napoleon, or Spanish galleons breaking up in a storm."

"So he gives you Saint Patrick's sermons and Queen Maeve's wiles against rows of King Henrys and Jameses?"

"That's right, and tales of Hugh O'Neil and Brian Boru against the English stories of Nelson and Cromwell."

Mrs. Connory's eyes grew dreamy. "I always loved the stories about Hugh O'Neil—such a man he must have been to steal his love, the daughter of his worst enemy, out from under the nose of her father."

I breathed in the fresh, salty odor of the baking bread and sighed. "It is much like Paris of Troy stealing Helen from the Greek King," I said. "Joe says that we have heroes and fools to match those of Homer. And poets to rant of them, too. To teil the truth, I don't think Joe cares much for any of the stories, Irish or Greek."

"Maybe we dream too much of past glory," Mrs. Connory said and went to test the bread for doneness, pressing the browning top with her fingers.

Later, Brendan rode with me back to Shannon Farm. The air was clear and frosty. Snow sugared the far off Galty Mountains.

"Have you been to Cahir, Maggie?" Brendan asked. He wore a brown cap that leaked his curls, making a blue-black frame to his face. When he smiled, I saw the tooth that he'd chipped falling from a stone wall that we'd been walking atop when we were children.

"Not for a very long time. I went with Grandfather when I was eight or nine, in Bridey's cart on some errand. We saw Bianconi coaches, giant carriages with four heavy wheels and eight great horses to pull them at a gallop all the way to Dublin." The horses had been lathered and blowing steam, each of them looking like a horse belonging to the giant Fomor. "I'd like to ride in one of those coaches some day."

"There are trains now. The Bianconi's are gone."

"Joe told me about the trains." I felt sorry for the loss of the coaches and horses, but I'd like to have seen a train belching smoke and striking sparks from the rails like the train in an advertising poster.

"What else does your brother tell you about Cahir?"

"He went there last month and left all the chores to Grandfather and me for a day and a half. Then he wouldn't tell me a thing about what he did there. He's no better than you in that way."

"Am I so difficult?"

"Oh, Brendan, will you never tell me about all those evenings at the mill with your father and Joe and the other men?"

"I told you some."

"And so did Joe and your mother. But not enough. I have the right to know. Your brother is always in Dublin or Cork, and when he comes home, Joe can't wait to be out the door of an evening. If treason is spoken, Joe's in danger. As are you and your father. That's what Grandfather says."

"Have you heard of the Monster Rallies going on all over Ireland?"

"You know our English schoolmaster doesn't allow us to speak of them, but I think they are all about Home Rule and against the English laws."

"And so they are. And that's what we talk about at the Mill as well. Would you like to go with me?"

"To the mill with the men?"

"To Cahir—where a Monster Rally is to form tomorrow. People will come from all over Tipperary, and Cork, too."

"Tomorrow is school."

"You'll miss it."

"Brendan . . . the danger! Grandfather and Joe would never let me go."

"The British dragoons have marched out from Cahir Castle and are off over the Vee of the mountains, chasing Fenians in Lismore Town. You'll see some of the greatest patriots in Ireland and hear all that you are so curious about."

"Still they would never allow me . . . "

"Then you won't tell them. You are the brave winner of the Galty Chase. You are fourteen years of age and will decide to do some things for yourself. You'll see the famous poet, Finnegan. And hear him, too. Maggie, you wouldn't believe the music of words until you . . . "

We were nearly to Shannon Farm, and Brendan had been talking the whole way, trying to shape his words into a picture of what tomorrow would be—the crowds, the babble, and the speakers, larger than life.

If we'd noticed the dragoons lounging beside the river, we might have ridden to avoid them, but as it was, we were already to the bridge before we saw the red coats, belted with white.

As we passed, Brendan on the outside, the men turned curious faces to me, a farm girl with fine boots on a splendid horse. One of them called, "Hey, lass, give us a kiss!"

I ducked my head, and my hair fell forward over my burning cheeks. Beside me, Brendan pulled back on Sultan's reins, his face pale with anger. He would have wheeled his horse and turned back to—to do what?

Would he attack the soldiers, a youth with fists against armed men?

I reached across to grab Sultan's bridle and kicked Peg. She surged ahead, pulling the bay into a trot beside her. "Brendan, please," I begged.

He tried to resist for a moment; then he rode with me, galloping over the bridge and the rest of the way to the farm.

At my gate, Brendan turned his white face to me. "You shouldn't have stopped me. They had no right."

"No right, Brendan, but the right of their guns. For all your brawn and temper, it would be no use to fight. And they are far from their English homes, after all, and bored and ignorant."

"Do you know how shamed I feel?" Brendan said. "A man should not have to . . . "

"It's all right," I said, leaning from my saddle to touch his sleeve. "Please don't think it matters." I dismounted and opened the gate, patting Peg to go through it without me.

I thought of Joe and how the gold had dragged at him as we came from Drummond's. "Brendan," I said, "I've made up my mind to go with you in the morning."

⊰ CHAPTER 16 ⊱

ON THE ROAD TO CAHIR

With great stealth, I slipped from my room and out the door without waking Joe or Grandfather, just as I had the night I'd dug my leprechaun trap in the Fairy Woods. Almost a year ago, that night was now at the other end of the world.

I took Bran with me to the shed and made him stay. The dog watched with mournful eyes as I led saddled Peg into the yard and left him behind.

Peg's ears worked back and forth, alert and wondering.

Brendan was waiting at the gate, standing beside Sultan. "Did they hear you?" he asked.

"No. I left them a note so they will know where I've gone. I didn't want to lie to them."

Brendan stood at Peg's neck and steadied her so that I could mount. Then he placed his hand over mine. "I'm glad you're coming with me," he said. His hand was warm and dry as though he'd recently held it over a hearth fire. The horses smelled like hay, and Brendan smelled like strong lye soap.

He mounted Sultan, and the horses pranced and shook their reins and snorted clouds of vapor into the early morning air. I understood their excitement, for I felt it myself.

I smiled, thinking ahead to Cahir and wondering what it would be like, beyond what Brendan had already told me. "I feel like a conspirator," I said, "someone wicked and daring to be leaving my home by dark."

"You are beginning the life of a revolutionary and will hide in caves the rest of your years!"

I laughed. We were playing a game with our words, but one that gave me a shiver, as though I was involved in a dangerous act. A brave girl riding a brave horse.

The sun came up behind thick winter clouds. The light it gave was somber. A dark day sometimes gave way to fine weather, but even if this one didn't, I counted it fair for being a day I would remember always.

As we passed between high rock walls, Brendan sang familiar tunes. But the words were Gaelic, and I could not follow their meaning. The sound was melancholy blended with gaiety, and I was content to hum along.

The fences opened to thatched cottages clustered in snug neighborliness, their chimneys acurl with heavy peat smoke. Sometimes a dog barked or joined us for awhile. Sometimes we passed a donkey cart or a scrubbed family, all headed toward Cahir.

Later and farther down the road, some of the walls fenced in sheep, and I called to Brendan, "Look at the cunning pink faces staring at us from their thick collars of wool."

Brendan looked at me speculatively, as though he was about to tell me something. He shook his head as if to shake away whatever thought he was having.

He began to sing again, and I asked him to teach me the songs.

"What? Irish and not sing, Maggie?"

"Oh, yes, we sing at home, but it's the language I don't know. Grandfather talks some in Gaelic to his friends of an evening over a glass of pocheen, but Joe and I have never learned. Schoolmaster calls Gaelic an inferior tongue to English, and he cracked little Tommy O'Brien on the knuckles for only a word or two on the playground."

Again Brendan shook off something he was about to say. Then we talked again of ordinary things, things of no more importance than his sister, Nan, going north to visit some cousins and how much my grandfather enjoyed his pipe of an evening.

For a moment we lost our conversation to Sultan's snorting and prancing at the far-off sight of sheep driven onto the road by a shepherd and his dog.

"Joe and I took coins from the Galty win to Drummond, asking to buy back the land." I blurted the information as if the words had decided of themselves to jump from my mouth. "It wasn't enough. But after two more wins with Pegasus, we'll have enough gold to tempt even Drummond, Joe thinks."

"Two more wins, is it? I wouldn't count on it, Maggie! No one has ever won three years with the same horse! Peg is a champ, but Cashel will not stumble next November. Sultan will run truer."

"There's more to the tale, though you know some of it already, Brendan. The penny that bought Peg—I came by it in the Fairy Woods. I believe it came from a leprechaun. I believe Peg has magic in her."

"Maggie, no!" A laugh began to crinkle Brendan's face, but disappeared. Maybe he saw the seriousness that I felt or was remembering the trader's words, *I'll give you this one for a leprechaun's penny*. Brendan must be remembering the look of surprise and cunning cross the trader's face as I dropped my coin into his hand.

"Is this true?" Brendan asked.

"I think so."

We pulled the horses to the side of the road while the sheep, bleating and raising dust, passed. The shepherd doffed his hat and greeted us with "Good day." We returned his greeting.

The horses tugged at their bridles and Brendan and I allowed them a trot up the hill. Once down the other side, Brendan nodded, and I responded with a cluck and kick of my heels to Peg's ribs. The horses flew out of their trot into a madcap gallop.

The strong legs of the horses carried us past a blur of stone fences overgrown with gorse and briar. Beyond, the Galty Range curved gently, icy mist swirling about the heads of the tallest peaks.

Sultan surged ahead for an instant, and I laughed in answer to the white flash of Brendan's teeth. I caught a glimpse of sky-blue eyes before the face turned and Brendan's hand shot back to slap the glistening rump of his horse. I loosened my grip on the reins and urged, "Let's give him a run, Peg. Let's fly!"

The horses stretched out to run. Their hooves sang on the hard dirt of the road and drummed thrillingly around curves and over grades. Their iron shoes rang against the random stones.

Tall and round as barrels, pigs appeared in front of us, bringing Brendan and me upright in our saddles.

"Pigs in the road!" I screamed, and the horses skidded in a swirl of dust and gravel.

The pigs squealed and snorted and Sultan whinnied, but none of the pigs was harmed. They trotted away, ears stiff with alarm.

We collapsed like sacks of potatoes onto our saddles, coughing and laughing at the averted catastrophe.

Brendan grabbed across space for Peg's rein to bring me closer. "Let's walk for awhile," he said, "and rest the horses."

We dismounted and walked for a long stretch of road, hardly able to see to the other side of the high rock walls. When we came to a particular gate, one that I sensed Brendan had been looking for, he led Sultan through it and told me to follow.

Brendan pointed to an empty rectangle of roofless walls.

"A poor broken house," I said.

"You have seen houses like this before?"

"I have. From the times of famine when whole families died."

"This one lost its roof only last year."

"But how? Where did the people go who lived here?" I followed him through an open doorway. Grass had begun to push through the hard-packed dirt that was the floor of the cottage. Once the two windows in the room had been glazed, but the glass had been carted away by someone, as had the cottage door and the planks and beams that had held the roof.

102

"It makes a nice shelter from wind for those *cunning* sheep you noticed."

I looked at him, still not understanding.

"The farmland of Ireland is for its people and their crops, Maggie, not for sheep."

I heard the bitterness in Brendan's tone that I heard often in Joe's words.

"But where did the people go?"

"Across the Irish Sea to England or the great Western Ocean to America, I imagine, the roofs pulled off the houses for unpaid rents."

"Deliberately pulled off?"

"So no other family could shelter there. The sheep are the new tenants for this land. They have no use for doors and windows. The landlord needs only a shearing knife to collect his rent."

It was only the second time I'd seen Brendan angry, his eyes now the blue of a darker sky. Something stirred in my blood, and I heard in my mind Grandfather's laments for his own "dear, darling sisters," transported to America and never heard of since.

"I think you should know, Maggie, Sir Henry is putting ever more pasturage aside for sheep. He's been a decent enough landlord up till now, not foreclosing at the slimmest excuse like some. But he won't be eager to sell land to Joe."

"Somehow he must be made to do that, Brendan."

"Maybe." He swung back to the saddle, as did I. Once again we were on the road to Cahir and the Monster Rally, Brendan no longer singing and I with more thoughts awhirl in my head than I'd ever had any single day in my life.

103

⊰ CHAPTER 17 ⊱

POETS AND PATRIOTS

The River Suir flowed broad and peaceful as we crossed over it. *Suir* meant "south" in Gaelic, and it was pronounced "shur." Brendan was right. I should know more than a few words of my native tongue.

The waters of the Suir riffled gently on either side. They produced not a gurgle we could hear above the clatter of the horses' hooves on the stones of the bridge. Ahead and to our right, the English garrison that was Cahir Castle rose tall and weathered, only a little scarred by the passage of centuries. In our land of ruined buildings, it stood stout and dark, but whole. I looked up from the bridge to the castle, searching for faces, fearing to see guns, but the castle stared back from its empty windows.

Only a lone soldier stood guard at the gate, but yesterday Brendan and I had met dragoons at the River Tar. If those two had been left behind, maybe others waited within the castle to rush out and arrest everyone at the rally. I voiced those fears to Brendan, but he assured me there would be no trap. The soldiers had been seen marching to Lismore Town on the other side of the mountains. The few soldiers remaining were no present threat even with their guns. Although their eyes would memorize what faces they could and report them later.

"Might the army return early?"

"Not a chance they can get back before this meeting closes and we are all on our safe ways home." His hands, strong and competent on Sultan's reins, reassured me as much as his words.

The bridge was thronged, and the throng funneled onto the road that passed in front of the castle and into the Town Square. I had never been in a crowd like this before—the Galty Meet had been small by comparison. I was glad to be above it on Peg's back, glad to have Brendan riding beside me, stirrup to stirrup.

I thrilled to the sights and sounds. Peg worked her ears and turned her head to me. I patted her neck.

"We're of like mind, you and me, girl. I feel both crushed and excited."

Someone was playing pipes in the Square. A blind harpist sat on the porch of the Cahir House Hotel plucking a tune different from the air the pipes were rasping. Men were singing and boys shouted. The square was large, paved with stones, and without a single tree. A small monument stood like a knob in the center. People jostled each other, some leading donkeys. Where I had once seen the lathered Bianconi horses and the huge passenger coaches, children raced and women stood with hands on their hips to gossip.

Gray shawls twisted on turning shoulders, and the crowd gave off the excitement of celebration. The few houses we passed could not have emptied out so many red-faced, merry people. Brendan had said they came from all over the county and from other counties as well. I breathed in the scene like air from a place as far away as the moon. Riding into this throng was much like plunging from a cliff into a wild sea.

"There must be hundreds!"

"Many hundreds, Maggie, maybe a thousand."

Three merry girls, wearing shawls and identical wool dresses, pulled steaming potatoes from heavy pails and offered them from gloved hands. They giggled and curtsied to Brendan when he reached from his saddle to give them each a penny for three potatoes that he knotted into his handkerchief.

Passing among the people, boys in knee britches of homespun pressed handbills into outstretched hands. Angry voices raised above the general hubbub to call for "home rule," a government for the Irish people, and an "end to rack-rents," the unfair price put on the land by greedy landlords.

"Down with the Union to England!" was the cry.

Over and over, "Land for the people!"

Danger was in the slogans. England had ruled Ireland and its people for centuries. They would not give them up easily.

The Square had seemed full. Now it brimmed with people, people shoulder to shoulder and hip to hip. Brendan and I backed our horses between two buildings and stood in front of them. While Peg and Sultan pulled at the few clumps of weedy grass growing against the walls of the buildings, I balanced on a stone step to see above the heads of this ocean of people. At one edge of the square stood the fine Cahir House Hotel, three stories tall. On the opposite side was a platform stage.

Every paving stone of the square now held two or three men and women.

"Do you want to move closer to the stage, Maggie?"

"I am scared enough already of being crushed to death." In truth, I felt a moment of panic at the thought. I was secure on my stone step but knew I would be unable to breathe if I stepped down from it. "Let's stay where we are."

Brendan handed me a potato, and I held it for a few minutes to warm my hands before eating it.

One by one, speakers took the stage. A mixed lot, they spoke as if the angels themselves had taken human voice. The one who introduced the rest was a giant man in a gray-green coat with a green handkerchief knotted at his throat. I had never seen so rough and yet so handsome a man, and I had never seen anyone dare to wear green—except Patrick and Brendan at the Galty— a challenge to Red Coats any time.

He called out, "We must have a return to an Irish Parliament in Dublin!" The fury of his words caused my bones to shiver. "We must have rents that are fair and fair means to acquire land."

Another speaker was Finnegan, the great poet. He was short and round, with lashing hair. When he spoke in Gaelic, the consonants and vowels of his angry words swept over the crowd like waves, smoothing out the rippling of the people. They were one face turned to watch his gestures. They were one ear cocked to catch the sounds of the poetry.

"I don't know what he says, Brendan," I whispered. "He sounds ferocious and sometimes sad."

"You are not the only one who doesn't understand her own language, Maggie," Brendan whispered. "The poems tell of injustice and cruelty, also of bravery and lives lost."

"I could listen to his voice forever. It cannot be true what Schoolmaster said—that Gaelic is an inferior tongue."

When Finnegan concluded his recitations, three strong men carrying cudgels hurried him from the stage and began to cross the square. The throng in front of them fell back on either side, opening to let the men pass, then closing behind them until they were safely into the Cahir House Hotel.

"What are they up to?" I asked, fearful for the poet's life.

"Those are his bodyguards, Maggie; Finnegan has a price on his head for his words. If he were captured, the one turning him in would receive a bounty. The British consider him a great traitor. Words are more powerful than guns."

Then, wonder of wonders, another who was handed up to the platform was a woman, a lady, dressed simply, in a blue skirt and white, pleated shirtwaist. I had seen ladies dressed so on race day at Drummond House. Simplicity meant quality. She was introduced as Lady Edwina Darcy.

She spoke softly in a rich contralto voice, her face a pale flower above her collar.

"There can be no justice for this land so long as laws come from across the sea," she said. "The same proved true for the Americans. They threw off the yoke of English rule. And so shall we." The people cheered when she finished.

Onto the stage stepped a young man to help her down.

"It's Patrick!" Brendan said.

Patrick escorted Lady Darcy from the stage and started with her through the crowd toward the hotel, where the poet had gone before her. But Patrick was no bodyguard with a cudgel. The eager crowd did not open easily to let him pass with Lady Darcy.

All eyes turned toward the two of them and all hands reached to touch the lady as if her skin and clothing would somehow bring them what they lacked. Nothing ill was intended, I'm sure, but I could see she felt stifled. A sudden surge of the crowd separated her from Patrick.

The panic I had felt earlier in my own dizzy brain I saw reflected on Lady Darcy's pale face. Those at the rear of the crowd were pushing. I feared greatly that she might be crushed. Without thinking, for I had used up all thoughts on the road to this place, I took a deep breath, grabbed Peg's reins, climbed upon her back, and urged her through the many bodies between the lady and me.

Brendan was right behind me for I heard Sultan snorting at the challenge.

"Make way," I shouted. "Make way."

Patrick fought his way back to Lady Darcy's side. When he saw us, he charged toward us, pulling the lady in his wake. When he reached us, he hoisted her behind my saddle. "Lady Darcy, meet Maggie Shannon" was the entire introduction he gave before he swatted Peg's rump and sent us in the direction he wanted us to go. Feeling fiercely proud, I rode with Lady Darcy through the crowd and right up the very stairs of the hotel.

There, Finnegan, followed by his bodyguards, pulled her from behind my saddle. The hotel stairs and the hotel porch served as a safe haven from the crowd, who had now returned their attention to the stage and

109

the next speaker. I dismounted and led Peg back down the stairs where Brendan and Patrick waited.

"Wait!" Lady Darcy's command turned me around. I gave Peg's reins to Brendan and came back to the porch.

"Maggie Shannon," she said, "I thank you for your quick action. I thought I would suffocate."

"I feared for you," I answered, biting my lip. "Suffocation has been much on my mind this afternoon."

"She is the girl of whom I told you, Edwina," Patrick said. "And this mare is the gallant horse she rode to her victory in the Galty Prize race."

"You are a brave girl, Maggie Shannon." Lady Darcy took my hand in her gloved one. Her eyes were a clear gray, and she had smooth brown hair and a mouth that shaped itself handsomely around her words as she complimented me upon my victory.

"Thank you, ma'am," I said, breathless. "It was a fine speech you gave."

"Did you think so? My husband would give a better one, but he is in London, trying to persuade his fellows in the English Parliament to heed the true and deserving petitions of our people."

"I wish more believed as Lord Darcy, Madam," Patrick said.

"There are some. Not all the Irish peerage have deaf ears and stony hearts. Not all we Protestant landlords are devils." Her eyes flashed with good humor, and I rejoiced that she was no longer frightened.

"Sometime you may want my help. Patrick knows our lands near Dublin. You would be welcome there." I heard once more the strength and purpose of the words she had delivered from the stage. I felt those qualities enter my own mind. Very much as though she had deliberately placed them there.

"Is that agreed, Maggie Shannon? I owe you something, and I would enjoy seeing you again in a more peaceful setting."

Others spoke before Brendan and I departed—a scholar, a tradesman, and a priest. But, whether cultured gentleman or country peasant, all spoke with unified passion and conviction. They spoke of an Irish flag and ownership of land for all Irishmen, an end to children being hungry in a bountiful country, and an end to the strongest and best of Ireland's people crossing the great ocean to escape oppression at home.

Some would have their messages cut short while they languished behind bars in Dublin Prison. Brendan had warned such had been the fate of others. I was glad again for his assurance that the soldiers were far from Cahir and could touch none of us here.

All the way home, my words burst—as the clouds above threatened to do—deluging Brendan with questions for which he had ready answers.

"What have the Darcys to gain, Brendan? They have lands and tenants the same as Drummond."

"Having lands and tenants does not automatically mean tyranny and rack rents, Maggie. The Darcys do not leach their tenants to enrich an estate in England, as many others do. They call Ireland home."

Brendan paused. I wished to interrupt but couldn't before he continued. "Do you find it strange then that my family are for home rule and land reform? We are landowners, too."

"No, Brendan," I began in another breathless torrent. "You and your father and mother are different. The mill hasn't made you rich like Sir Henry, and

111

besides, don't you and your brother bear the names of the saints themselves?" I was little more than babbling in my attempt to tell Brendan what I felt.

Soon he was laughing at me. I turned hot and angry as I tried to speak above his mirth, until he pulled Sultan closer to Pegasus and laid a rough but gentle hand over my mouth.

"Maggie Kathleen Shannon, you are turning me dizzy with your blab. Hush now."

I quieted, but he did not remove his hand until his horse danced him away from me. "We will be friends, Maggie, for a long while," he whispered.

We rode the rest of the way home in the dark, the misty air carrying enough light to guide our way. Brendan's words still warmed my soul, and I wondered if his hand had marked my mouth, for I felt the touch of it still.

⊰ CHAPTER 18 ⊱

AN UNWELCOME REMINDER

Grandfather and Joe greeted me, anxiety etched
into both their faces.

"A young girl alone on the road to Cahir and
taking part in treasonous goings on," Joe chided. "Out
after dark! What could you be thinking of."

"I was with Brendan," I said.

"Making two fools, not just one! Grandfather is
nearly ill with worry, and I, angry enough to strap you if
it were my duty."

"I'm truly sorry for that," I said, lowering my eyes. I
was sorry for their feelings, though I could not make
myself sorry for going. "But the rally, Grandfather and
Joe, I can only wish I'd had you both with me. It was a
marvel, and I am different because of it."

Gradually, Joe eased up and Grandfather started at
me with questions. Over and over, I had to tell what I'd
heard and what I'd seen, exactly as it had happened.

113

Joe remained silent, but I could tell he was eager to hear. I saw again in his face the new respect for me that had come to him since the Galty Chase.

After the first night, no more was said, but certain words and sights played in my mind to the accompaniment of my daily chores, my studies, and the evenings by the fire. Lady Darcy's fine gray eyes and her kind words, ". . . you must call on me," often came to me, and I wondered how I might ever need help from so fine a person.

I saw again the lashing hair of the poet and the green scarves circling the necks of the speakers. I felt the crush of the crowd and heard the creak of the bagpipes and the thrum of the harp. Once more, pigs appeared and sent the horses prancing to a stop on the road to Cahir. Again I felt Brendan's hand against my mouth.

The ride to Cahir, the ride back, and the sights and sounds of the rally had stretched me, as the passing of the vernal equinox would soon stretch the daylight hours.

One February evening, Mrs. Connory sat beside me on a bench before the Connory hearth. We had both been stitching on different ends of a bed sheet, but now I stopped, holding my needle in mid-air.

"Before Brendan took me to the rally, I felt that every new thing I was told at school or saw with my eyes was being crammed into a head already full," I said. "But now I feel space within my whole body, empty and waiting to be filled. Do you know what I mean, Mrs. Connory? I listen more carefully and see more than I used to. I want to know things and do things, though I'm not sure what."

Mrs. Connory held my end of the sheet to inspect it. "Have you thought of going further in school, Maggie?" she asked.

"I'm already in school longer than anybody. Even Brendan is there just to help Schoolmaster."

"Dublin has schools. You could be a teacher, Maggie."

"Oh, I couldn't leave Grandfather and Joe, or Pegasus!"

"Not now, perhaps, but one day," Mrs. Connory said, and I could tell she was thinking something out, deciding how to say it. "The lady you met—Lady Darcy; she noticed you, Maggie. She might help. She and her husband have influence. They've been a great help to Patrick."

I sat, troubled by Mrs. Connory's words. The name of Dublin conjured only danger in my mind. Sure, there must be a great cathedral there and things precious to my people, but Dublin was the seat of English power and so to be feared.

Mrs. Connory was quick to drop her sewing and fetch tea for us both, quick to turn the conversation. "And what is going on with your brother, Maggie? How is Joe?"

"He's looking forward to spring. He hopes for two calves, this year."

"Two calves! Oh, wouldn't that be grand? I hope so."

"One to be fattened and sold, one we'll fatten and butcher for ourselves and our neighbors—some have been good to us in lean years."

"Your brother is due some good fortune."

"He's also beginning to plan how he can persuade Sir Henry to part with some of his acres. If Pegasus wins again, we will have more gold—perhaps it will make a difference."

"Speaking of the race coming up, will that skirt we fixed last year still do?" Mrs. Connory motioned for me to stand and then shook her head. "No, it will not. You've been stretching taller and changing your shape. We'll have to get to work on your clothes. Can the skirt you're wearing be lengthened? Let me see the hem. You'll soon turn fifteen; won't you?"

"You are good to me, Mrs. Connory." Yes, I'd noticed what Mrs. Connory had. I was indeed growing, in more ways than the stretching I felt in my mind.

"You are good for *me*, Maggie. It's lonesome now that our Nan is in the north helping my cousin with her children. I'm glad for your company."

In springtime the lazy-beds needed preparing, and I took a few days from school to knife potato eyes into hillocks of earth, sparing Grandfather, who tired more easily this year than last. The anniversary of finding Peg came also, along with daffodils, softer days, and the hoped-for calves, two of them this year, a great reason to rejoice.

Summer meant taking the cows to the far pastures each day, away from the fields where they had eaten winter grasses. Those manure-enriched fields must now be used for planting oats and rye.

I used the time watching the cows and the two small bullocks to groom Pegasus and read from my book of Greek legends, its cover frayed from the many hands before mine that had held it, its pages greasy from use. I practiced saying to Peg the Gaelic words that Brendan had taught me, and the mare swiveled her ears in appreciation of the musical language.

I went over and over in my mind the route of the Galty Steeplechase. I scratched faithful Bran behind the ears and planned my strategy for the next race.

Sometimes, as now, I leaned against Pegasus' bronze side, looked across the pasture to the grazing cows, and spoke to the mare from a well of hope and doubt.

"I'll not be so reckless with you, Peg," I said. I felt the ripple of muscles along her back as the mare curved her long neck to nuzzle my arm. *It's all right*, she was saying. *We handled the course*.

I touched Peg's velvet muzzle and rubbed the short, coarse hairs on her nose. "Oh, Pegeen," I said, thinking back nearly a year to the last race. "It was madcap, no reason to the running. I let you fly at the hurdles, wild and careless, as if we had nothing to lose. It wasn't that I didn't value you, but only that I didn't understand the danger. I hadn't seen others go down over the tree stumps and fences." I used Peg's halter to pull the great head against my own cheek.

She flicked her ears forward and pawed the ground eagerly.

"And then I felt the magic about the leprechaun's penny. Did I think that magic surrounded us with safety? No matter. You aren't to be handled like that again. This year we'll plan and be ready."

True to my words, I spent hours, after bringing in the cows, leading Peg over the course, sometimes with Brendan, sometimes alone. I showed Peg the hurdles from all positions, showed her the other side of the barriers, the bog and water-filled ditches, the sudden dips and rises. I showed her the steep hills and the hard road.

117

We tried the jumps again, at different speeds and from different positions.

In August, my fifteenth birthday came and went, with school beginning shortly thereafter. I could begin to look forward to November and Peg's second Galty chase.

Then, rain began on the eleventh of October and fell nearly daily until the race. It made soup of the bog and turned the ground into a slippery, gully-filled track.

The day before the race, the sun tried to undo some of the rain's mischief, and the day of the race was dry, if not cloudless. I led Peg around the paddock at Drummond House, mixing with the other riders and officials before the race. Straw covered the ground, but the surface was still sodden.

Sir Henry Drummond rode up to me on his strong gray gelding. He was dressed in fawn-colored riding pants with boots of inky black, and he spoke to me courteously, almost as though I were an equal.

"Maggie Shannon," he said, "it appears you plan to win again with your tinker's horse. The mare looks stronger and more graceful than ever."

"Thank you, sir," I answered.

"I remember your win last year. I've never seen the race run so well—though it was favorites of mine that you beat."

"Peg is a brave and canny horse for sure," I agreed. "She's ready again." I patted Peg's shoulder and felt the springy flesh and muscles with pleasure.

Sir Henry switched a fly from his horse's mane with a white-gloved hand. "You and your brother haven't forgotten my offer to buy Pegasus. Have you, Maggie?" he said.

118

I was startled, for, in truth, nothing was further from my mind. Now, the memory flooded back. My blood heated as I remembered the day in Drummond's office when Joe had made his offer, his humiliation when he was refused. Instead Sir Henry had offered to buy what was priceless—beautiful Peg.

The landowner smiled without showing his teeth. "Well, perhaps you have forgotten," he said, "but if your need is ever such that guineas of mine could ease the burden . . . "

"Sir, it's guineas aplenty we have since the last race," I said proudly. "Guineas we would gladly part with for the chance to buy back our farm."

Sir Henry pulled at his horse's reins and began to back him away. "Maggie, it wouldn't be sensible for me to carve into Drummond Estate to satisfy your brother's need to be a landowner. It would be against my best interests and the tides of destiny. You are safe enough here. I don't intend to throw my tenants off the land. Use your coins to buy a pig or some new dresses. Increase your well-being by selling me Pegasus."

The fire in my blood must have sent sparks to my eyes, for Sir Henry tipped his hat and completed his horse's turn away from me. "Perhaps you'll change your mind," he said over his shoulder, leaving me with a sinking heart even as the starter called the contestants to get ready for the race.

The enemy, I thought, as I had thought that day in Sir Henry's office. As I would think again before my life changed forever.

⊰ CHAPTER 19 ⊱
VICTORY FLAGS

On the day of my second Galty Race, Patrick was in Dublin looking for new markets for the Connory share of the grain they ground at Connory Mill, and Brendan rode speedy Cashel. My friend made a fine sight on the black horse. His blue eyes flashed and his nearly black hair curled wild at the edges of his cap. I became conscious of my own usually unruly mop. This morning I'd brushed it to shine with Peg's like copper and had pulled it behind my ears, tying it at the nape of my neck with a green ribbon. Only a few strands strayed to tickle my forehead.

"Can you handle your mare in this swamp of a course, Maggie Kathleen?" Brendan asked as he steadied eager Cashel for the start.

"Better than some, I imagine," I answered, giving him a sideways glance as I did some steadying of my own.

Sir Henry Drummond receded from my mind, and my spirits lifted.

"If you want, I'll get Patrick back from Dublin to take her over the jumps for you."

"No, thank you," I teased back. "Just beware you don't let Cashel get mud in his eyes when Peg gallops past."

"Cashel and I will mind ourselves."

The starter called for the riders to be ready and raised his flag at the end of the pasture.

"I wish you well, Brendan," I said. "I wish both of us could be winners."

"Maybe not today, but someday," he answered, beguiling me with his smile.

The horses pranced and trotted from all corners of the field, some not yet headed toward the starter and crabbing or circling fractiously. But by the time the flag flashed down, all were ready to bolt toward the first fence. Once again, Peg and I became part of a general crush as the horses cleared the wooden bars in tight bunches.

With horses around us slipping and skidding, I took care to keep Peg from being forced from the track to the shortcut Brendan and I had taken before. The course was far too muddy for shortcuts. I kept her to the drier part of the roadway, where it curved downhill. She broke free of the pack at the path to the stumps.

Her muscles bunched and stretched beneath my heels, and she sailed the stumps safely, alone in the lead. Behind, horses squealed and men shouted. Some must have gone down, and I prayed Cashel hadn't been one of them. I heard Brendan urging the speedy stallion and knew they were safe, but by the frustration in his voice, I knew they had been blocked by other riders.

121

Ahead lay the bog, swollen and soupy from all the rain. I rejoiced at Peg's brilliant instincts, as she found firm footing to gain an even greater lead.

The road curved away from the bog, giving me a chance to see the followers. Brendan and Cashel were neck and neck with Mr. Fergus O'Hanlon's strong brown horse, but even they were many, many horse-lengths behind. So far, the race had been easier than I had dared hope.

Then, at the last of the fences past the bog, Pegasus took off grandly and soared cleanly over the briars that crowned the fence, but, on the other side, she slid in mud and stumbled, throwing me over her shoulder.

I landed in a great slosh of mud that coated me up and down one side with black muck, but I gained my feet quickly. Carried away by the momentum, Peg now returned to my side. I ignored the mess and my jolted bones, pulled myself onto the saddle, caught up the reins, and swung my leg over her back.

"Fly, Pegasus, fly," I urged. "We mustn't let them catch us."

Peg began the climb toward the stone wall and the pond at the finish. Cashel was still a length back with the brown falling further behind. Through my hands, that were knotted into her mane and pressed against her neck, I felt the pound of her great heart. The bellows of her lungs filled and expelled laboriously. Both my hands and her neck were drenched with lather. Her hooves drummed the dry stretch toward the finish.

Over my shoulder, I glanced Cashel running with all the great speed for which he was known, but Peg continued on, taking the final fences, once more breaking the string of victory flags at the finish.

I collapsed over Peg's neck. I gave her an enormous hug, then pulled back on the reins to bring the mare to a canter, then to a trot and, finally, to a walk.

"You did it, girl," I whispered. "The race and soon the farm. You did it. Oh, you did it!"

Arms reached to pull me from the horse, and hands reached to pat Peg's dripping sides, others to take the reins and lead the mare about, to be petted and praised while she cooled down.

Brendan clasped me in a muddy embrace, while all around swirled congratulations for the fine run and the glorious hurdling.

"You and Peg were brilliant, Maggie," Brendan said. "I'm sorry for your misfortune."

"We were hemmed in early. I'd have beaten you with Cashel if I could. Next year you may not be so lucky."

Did Brendan truly understand how the race was more than the gold and the trophy? It all was for Grandfather and Joe.

My eyes found Pegasus, proud and beautiful, as children led her about. *Pegasus, you are the treasure of my heart, and you, too, are worth more than glory and gold.*

Then, my eyes, just above the line of Brendan's shoulder, spotted Joe across the sea of well-wishers. My heart rose up, ready to share my happiness with him, but as he came closer, I saw the lines of worry stamped upon his face. He was fighting the crowd to get to me, his eyes desperately seeking mine while the milling of children and others cut him off. I knew without a word from his lips.

"Grandfather!" I said and twisted out of Brendan's arms. All my joy clotted into grief.

⊰ CHAPTER 20 ⊱

GRANDFATHER

We took Grandfather home in O'Sullivan's cart behind the O'Sullivan donkey. Friends had given ragged blankets, brought to the race to sit on, and some they put beneath Grandfather, tumbling more over and about him. If the cart's jolting bothered him, he failed to show it. His eyes were closed, and his face was slack and pale.

"Take him home and keep him quiet," the nursemaid to Sir Henry's children had told me before we left. "It's a stroke, but I believe he'll recover with good care and patience."

"It was like this with my father," Mr. Fergus O'Hanlon had told me. "Pray God he'll recover, for my own father did not."

The British Magistrate, who had come from Cahir to attend the race, promised to send Dr. Casey, Cahir's only physician, as soon as the doctor returned from a brief fishing trip.

I walked with Joe beside the cart, constantly tucking blankets and talking to Grandfather in worried tones. I told him he needed some good stew and bread. I assured him I would be by his side every moment.

Peg walked placidly as a plow horse, tied to the back of the cart. Her great victory lay forgotten in the minds of her family, but if it bothered her, she didn't show it. The attitude of her ears and head said that she shared our worry.

"It must have been the sun," I said to Joe.

"Maggie, the sun hasn't shone for a month," he answered.

"It was the excitement. We should have known he wasn't up to it."

"We had no way of knowing that. If we had, do you think you could have kept him from watching you and Peg?"

We carried him carefully into the cottage with the help of two O'Sullivans and Brendan Connory. We dragged his bed from the bedroom, set it in front of the fire, and laid Grandfather on it.

"Is he warm enough, do you think?" I said.

"Touching and poking him as you do, you may bruise him," Joe answered, but, though his words were testy, I knew he grieved and worried as much as I did.

After finding we could no longer both remain awake for the long hours of days and nights that now blended together for us, we took turns sitting beside the quiet bed. Though Grandfather's eyes were open, he breathed only faintly. When a spoon was held to his lips, he sipped reflexively.

When both Joe and I were awake, one must be tending to the cows and horses. Pegasus must be exercised, and Brendan came daily and took on this responsibility. Neighbors were in and out. Brendan was always bringing another armload of peat for the fire. Mrs. O'Sullivan or Mrs. Connory or another was always adding to the steaming kettle a carrot, a piece of mutton, an onion or cabbage leaves. A cup of tea on a saucer would be placed in my hands while I was urged up the stairs for a nap.

Joe waked me for my turn to watch. "Any change?" I would ask.

"None that I can tell for sure, though once he moved his hand over the quilt."

I looked for a light in Grandfather's eye the day Fergus O'Hanlon placed the Galty trophy on the hearth so that Grandfather might catch the gleam on the raw engraving.

Though he looked toward it, no one was sure he saw the cup, but his fingers trembled ever so slightly, as if they wished to trace the words I read to him: *Shannon's Pegasus 1869*, newly cut on the mellow silver below *Shannon's Pegasus 1868*.

"It's two wins toward the three, Grandfather," I told him again and again. "The cup will be ours to keep after another year. And we'll have the farm, too. I know we will." And all the time I thought about how hollow the winning would be without Grandfather to share the triumph of our dreams come true.

November passed and Christmas occurred without distinction, except that the long-promised doctor visited

Grandfather from Cahir to pronounce that he "was doing well, and should recover within the year."

Joe took an extra armload of peat logs with him when his turn came to leave Grandfather's sickbed and go to chapel, an offering to repay the many kindnesses of the congregation and in thanks for the doctor's prediction.

When my turn came, I rode Pegasus, allowing myself the guilty pleasure of enjoying the ride. Peg pulled at her bit and insisted on a wild run. *It had been too long. It was fine to be carrying Maggie once more.*

In the days following, though he was yet to speak, Grandfather grew stronger and sometimes sat in his chair to be fed. The right side of his mouth drooped, but each day the droop became straighter. His right hand, that had hung useless, now held tightly to the edge of his blanket.

Brendan came often after meals to read to Grandfather from the Greek texts he loved, tell him legends and sing songs in Gaelic.

"I do believe he understands, Brendan. These times are so good for him," I said. *And they are good for me also,* my mind added secretly.

"You can sing with me, Maggie," Brendan told me. "You will soon have your own language as natural as the other you speak."

"There are few I could speak to in Gaelic and be understood," I said.

"Oh, you might be surprised. I hear that on the Dingle and near Galway it's spoken on the streets when there are no soldiers about."

He helped me, too, with calculations and studies of Irish and world history, so that I wouldn't suffer from staying out of school to minister to Grandfather. He told me with pleasure in his voice that I had a good mind.

127

"Your country will have need of you," Brendan told me. "Someday, the English will be gone, and we will need our own magistrates and prime ministers and teachers."

"I would love to be a teacher."

"And you'll be one of the best, Maggie, if you choose that way. Or maybe you'll help me manage the mill, for I'm the only one of my family who wishes to follow my father on his land."

I looked up quickly to see if Brendan teased me but could not be sure that the light in his eye was amusement or challenge. Since I couldn't tell what he meant and would not have known how to answer in any case, I turned to stir the fire and reposition the dinner potatoes with a long wooden spoon.

In the early days of spring, Grandfather improved enough to feed himself and drag his weakened body from bed to a nearby chair. While Joe and I planted, Grandfather sat bundled in blankets in the yard, Bran at his side.

A neighbor boy, hired for a few pennies, took the cows to pasture and the milk to the Big House.

"I'm going back to Drummond," Joe announced one day over tea. We sat with Mrs. Connory who had brought soda bread with precious raisins baked in. Grandfather sat apart, nearer the fire.

Mrs. Connory and I looked up, surprised.

"What will you say?" I asked. "Do you think he will change his mind?"

"I'll offer him both prize purses. He must never think we will give up. Maybe he will tire of saying no."

"Will there ever be such a softening of his heart?"

"There must be, Maggie, before my own breaks."

"Maybe we should wait till we have a third purse."

128

Joe turned to Grandfather. "What do you say, Grand-da? Shall we wait?"

We looked at Grandfather, hoping for a response, in time to see tears build in the old eyes.

"The farm," Grandfather said haltingly, his first words since he had been stricken.

I rushed to kneel beside my grandfather and hug his knees, my head in his lap. All these months since race day, even the days warmed by Brendan's visits and Grandfather's improved condition, fear had been a hard kernel pressed against my heart. Now, his tears and words told me that he was back in my world and all my efforts with Peg counted for something.

"Thanks be to God," said Mrs. Connory, and Joe smiled broadly and thumped the table.

⤳ CHAPTER 21 ⤲

A DESPERATE WAGER

Mrs. Connory stayed with Grandfather so that
Joe and I could go to Drummond's Big House.
"Will you take me, too, Joe?" I had asked,
fearful to go, but too curious to be left behind.

"It's because of you we have the coins" had been his
answer.

We walked silently together, full of our happiness
over Grandfather's first words since the race, full of our
hope.

But, once inside Drummond's office with its
gleaming brass and crystal, we were faced with much the
same scene as before. Drummond refused to consider the
two bags of coin.

"Then we offer the third purse," I said boldly as the
thought came to me. "For Pegasus will run next year to
bring the trophy to Shannon Farm."

"I can't settle for such a promise," Sir Henry answered.

I felt defeated, but beside me Joe was unhooking the purses from his belt.

He dropped the two on Sir Henry's desk. "The coins are all there except for three spent from the first bag and two held back from the second. By themselves they are more than enough for our few poor acres. But, as my sister has said, we pledge you the third also."

Here Sir Henry interrupted with a quick shake of his head.

"There is more," Joe said. I looked up in wonder to know what he would say. "If Pegasus should fail to win, you have these two purses and we get nothing." Joe placed his hand over mine.

My heart jumped at his boldness. Would the gamble tempt Sir Henry? I watched him as he picked up one bag and then the other to heft the weight, but absently as though he was no more concerned than if he hefted pebbles.

Suddenly he moved the two bags closer together and stood up. "All right," he said. "We will bargain. I'll take your offer, but with further conditions." He flicked his glance over me, then looked straight into Joe's eyes. I shuddered to see the coldness of the stare.

"If Pegasus loses, you forfeit the two bags and also the mare. In return I'll give passage to emigrate for the three of your family. You can sail to America and build a new life."

I gasped. "Emigrate! We would not!"

"Why not?" Sir Henry asked, continuing his stare into Joe's eyes. "It will be a new chance in a land made up of people just like you. Many have made their way there. Your land is little good for farming anyway.

131

Tipperary is better suited to grazing. I need your land for sheep and horses. I can afford to be generous."

"It's a deal," said Joe quietly. "But without the horse."

"Without the horse there is no deal. Pegasus will prosper in my pastures. She will produce colts to carry on her name. I promise never to sell her or let her want. She is the finest mare I've ever seen."

"Never!" Joe said.

"Think, man! She would be no good to you if you lose your farm and emigrate. I'll leave you two alone to discuss it." So saying, Sir Henry stood up from his mahogany desk and left the room through windowed doors. Before the doors closed on his back, the glorious scents of roses and lavender wafted inside. A contrast to the sour feeling in my stomach.

Joe reached for the bags, ready to go home.

I stopped his arm with my hand.

"He's right, Joe," I said. "You were willing to wager the gold we have now along with that yet to come. If we lose next time, even without the wager, he'll turn Shannon Farm over to sheep and force us to emigrate. We'd have no use for Pegasus then. But we won't lose. She is unbeatable, Joe; you saw her. I know it. You must believe it, too!"

Joe's face showed his misery and his rising hope. "I can't let you promise that, and how could we dare such a wager without Grandfather's knowing? We were wrong to have gone as far as we did. I repent that."

"No, we were right to make the offer, and we dare not tell Grandfather. When we win will be soon enough. Worry would be bad for him now."

When Sir Henry returned, he carried a lovely bouquet of yellow and pink roses in his arms. He laid the flowers on the desk and stood waiting, while the perfume of the roses filled the luxurious room with further luxury.

Joe extended his hand. "Done," he said. "We'll take the risk. The gold and Pegasus against the farm. And I'll have that in writing, please."

Sir Henry took the hand Joe offered. "Done."

When the landlord had written the contract and he and Joe had signed it, Joe took my elbow and steered me from the room, leaving behind the heavy bags of gold.

⇥ CHAPTER 22 ⇤

HIGH HOPES

Grandfather's words began to flow much as before, more slowly perhaps, but with only a bit of slurring. By August, he had reclaimed some of his simpler chores such as mending and cooking.

He walked with the aid of a gnarled stick, shuffling to the barn to lay a hand on Peg or Bridey, to offer a bit of hay to one of the cows. He watched me as I milked Iris. "Not too much, Maggie," he said. "Leave some for the calf."

"Don't worry, I'll not let Iris's baby go hungry—nor Daisy's either. Look at Daisy's calf, Grandfather, isn't she beautiful?"

"Truly. I'm glad Joe will keep her. She's a fine heifer."

"It's the extra rye from Joe's high acre that makes it possible."

"Have you named her, Maggie?"

"She's Violet, Grandfather, and a great favorite of Pegasus. See how they nuzzle one another?"

The heifer pushed and bellowed at the mare as if the horse was her mother, and Peg touched her nose to the little one's side.

"Things are getting better for us, Grandfather."

"Yes, that's sure." He stopped, struggling for the words he wanted, then said, "Piggies squealing in the yard . . . two calves . . . beautiful Peg . . . sturdy Bridey . . . cockcrow and his hens . . . plenty to eat . . . the rent and the gold coins, too."

Joe and I hadn't told Grandfather that the gold coins now resided at Drummond House or that the future of the farm itself and our destiny lay beside those purses. Why did he need to know? It was enough to tell him that Drummond had consented to sell once the third purse was ours.

"I hadn't thought it possible," Grandfather had said. "And after the race, what will you do, Maggie?"

"Maybe I would like to go further in school."

"And Brendan?"

"He will stay at the mill. He loves the land and the business."

"It's not what I meant. You've told me only what I already know. What about Brendan and you? You'll soon be sixteen; he is eighteen. I've seen the way Brendan looks at you. He'll soon have marriage on his mind."

"He hasn't said so." I turned away. "In any case, there's plenty of time to think about that."

"And Joe. Perhaps with the farm ours, Joe will consider a wife. There must be a girl in County Tipperary he'd like to bring to Shannon Farm."

I thought of Nan Connory's dimpled face and Joe's coloring at the mention of her name. "Maybe," I said. In

135

front of me stretched a misty future, mapped with unknown paths and faces, but I turned my mind from those far wanderings to consider only the closer goals. Pegasus would race and win in November. All other dreams depended on that one.

Hoofbeats pounding the road by the cottage interrupted my thoughts. I looked out to see a tall rider on a handsome gray horse outrunning a swirl of dust. He shouted a "hello" as he raced by.

"Young Patrick Connory coming home," Grandfather said. "Taking a chance to show his face. The magistrates and soldiers always know."

I watched as Patrick took the gray over neighboring walls to shortcut cross-country to the mill. He rode as madcap as ever, sure of his mount and his own horsemanship. I watched until I could see him no more.

"He's done no wrong, Grandfather, only speak out against the British landowners who put tenants off their land without cause."

"Speaking out's the same as shooting, in the eyes of the magistrates."

"But Patrick doesn't believe in violence, Grandfather. Brendan tells me Patrick and Lord Darcy and the others wish to change the hearts of the rulers through their ears."

"Then they'll have to find ears and hearts where none have been known to grow," Grandfather said with bitterness.

"Oh, Grandfather," I said. "I wish I understood life. I only know that Peg has brought us happiness."

⊰ CHAPTER 23 ⊱

PARTY FOR A SIXTEENTH BIRTHDAY

"Here it is, from Grandfather and myself." Joe thrust a package into my hands. It was wrapped in crinkly white paper and tied with string, a sixteenth birthday present, the first gift I could remember other than the divided skirt from Mrs. Connory and, once, a doll Grandfather had fashioned for me from a piece of wood. I slid my fingers between the folds of tissue trying to discover what was inside. How could a soft square package make me feel so dizzy?

"You can open it, you know. It's for you," Joe said.

From my chair, I looked across the table at Joe and at Grandfather. I tugged gently at the string on the package, but still could not pull the paper off. Surely, it was a dream. The paper would turn to dust in my hands.

Then the paper fell away, and the skirt—for it was a skirt—unfolded and fell across my knees. The fabric was heavy, yet light—smooth, but rough—blue and brown, also green, so lovely that tears softened my sight of it. I gripped it tightly and rose to hug first Joe and then Grandfather, the skirt crushed between our bodies.

"Oh, Joe. Oh, Grandfather. It's beautiful! I'm so happy. I feel like I've been touched by fairy magic."

"Yes, well, it cost enough," said Joe roughly, but I knew that his heart was as full as mine.

We shared the miracle of Pegasus winning at the Galty, the joy of Grandfather's recovery from his stroke, and the promise that our farm would once more belong to Shannons. The race was only weeks away, and Peg was strong and eager.

"There's more," said someone at the door, and into the room spilled people to fill the cottage—Connorys, Mr. and Mrs., Nan back from the north, Brendan and Patrick; O'Sullivans, six; and O'Briens, five. Bottles and cakes sprang from baskets, also ribbons and a new shawl, the gift of Patrick, Nan and Brendan. In presenting it to me, Brendan brushed my cheek with his lips. I blushed, and the younger children giggled. I ran off to Grandfather's room to change into the new clothes.

We sang in English and Gaelic, and although we had no harp or pipes, yet we did well enough, and the full masculine voices of Brendan and Patrick vibrated thrillingly.

As he sang, Brendan's eyes engaged mine so that the words of the ballads spoke straight to my heart.

Later, the O'Brien girls chanted a lilting rhythm that all danced to. As I whirled to the music, I caught sight, reflected in my mother's mirror that hung by the door, of blue and green ribbons flying; also, of my hair shining with copper lights. I wore the new shawl over my blouse, tucked in the waist of the new skirt. The green of it would bring out the green of my eyes and complement the heather colors of the skirt. I had a new thought about myself, that I might be pretty, not like Lady Darcy or Nan Connory, but pretty enough.

I was handed back and forth among the men and boys in a carefree reel, and I jigged with Nan Connory and one of the O'Sullivans. With Brendan's firm hand at my waist, I closed my eyes and felt the spinning of the dance and the spinning of the earth as well.

When we fell back, exhausted from the dancing and singing, Mr. O'Sullivan produced a brown bottle of pocheen. He uncorked it and passed it among the men. The young men and some of the grown women drank beer, while I, the other young women, and the children had tea with hot milk. The cakes vanished while stories were told.

Some told about the "good people" and their fairy magic. One told a story about an old man we all knew who nearly drowned in a bog, led there by fairy pipers. We heard of babes carried off and never again seen, though at night infant voices called for their mothers through the sighing wind. What a long time ago it seemed that I had won Pegasus with a leprechaun's penny. Had that really happened? I began to wonder.

Then the stories became those of Irish heroes of the past. Grandfather told again the story of the first Galty Race, and in my mind, Brian Boru and his horse Ossian once more defeated Fomor and his fire-breathing mount. Next came tales of the Munster kings and of brave Queen Maeve, later of the patriot Wolfe Tone, whom the O'Briens' grandfather had actually seen on the streets of Dublin early in the century. Finally they talked of young men gone to dark prisons because they spoke for Ireland.

I thrilled to the tales and rubbed my fingers over the hem of the lovely skirt and thought I had never been happier, nor ever sadder. I leaned against Mrs. Connory, as if the woman were my mother, and watched Joe slide glances at Nan Connory. I smiled into Brendan's eyes as he argued outrageously with his brother. If one were handsomer than the other, I couldn't detect it.

When the evening light failed, Joe lit precious candles, and the talk became serious. The men discussed rents and closings. Many cottages in nearby Ballylooby had been pulled down and families sent moving, the lucky ones to America to become farmers, or servants in fine houses, saving their coins to buy passage for their kin. Mrs. O'Sullivan spoke proudly of a cousin who had become a policeman, a "protector" of the people, she had called him, not an "oppressor" like the constables here.

Patrick, just back from Dublin, said that the British Parliament in London talked of laws to make the landlords soften the rents and allow tenants to buy land if they could. Talk was talk, yet it gave hope. So far, Drummond was standing fast against selling any of his land to tenants.

Still, Drummond hadn't evicted anyone, except poor Finney O'Rourke who had farmed the rocks above the heather with no success—and him with eight children. And that was sad, but at least passage had been given to the three oldest, so money would be sent from a place called Boston—if the rest didn't starve first. One of the O'Briens said the O'Rourkes were sheltering themselves outside town and living on handouts. Soon they'd be wandering the roads like Gypsy tinkers.

"You ride to O'Rourkes tomorrow, Maggie," Grandfather said. "Take a basket of potatoes. It won't right the wrong, but it will fill their bellies."

One of the O'Sullivans said, "It isn't always the ones on the meanest land whose houses are tumbled; often as not it's the home of someone who has prospered. Wouldn't a landlord rather have his lambs and ewes graze the bottoms rather than the hillside?"

And on it went until a young O'Brien who had been left home appeared to say that a dragoon, a red-coated soldier, had come to his door looking for someone named Dan O'Shaunessy, but it was the guess of the young O'Brien that the dragoon was scouting about for an illegal meeting of Home Rulers.

I looked to Patrick. Was it for him the dragoons searched? Could a birthday party become an "illegal meeting?"

The neighbors hastened to say goodbye. Patrick gave a small kiss to the cheek of "the birthday girl" and quickly left. The hooves of his horse pounded across the yard before the others had gathered up their baskets and shawls.

Mr. and Mrs. Connory lingered longest over their goodbyes, and Brendan led me outside to admire the stars in the moonless sky. In that moment while I stood outside the door with Brendan, he put a hand at my waist and another at the back of my neck and pulled me to him. He kissed me full on the mouth as I had once spied Joe kissing Nan outside the mill. Then, before I could react, the kiss was over. Brendan spun me into the light of the doorway and kissed me again, this time lightly on the cheek, a "goodbye" as he pulled on his cap and left with his mother and father.

I watched my friends depart. Lanterns bobbed up the road in the hands of O'Sullivans and O'Briens as they walked home. Down the road, toward the river, rode the Connorys. My lips felt warm and oddly swollen as if

141

a single kiss had changed their shape forever. I yearned to pull Brendan back to me, to once more feel his arms drawing me close.

⊰ CHAPTER 24 ⊱

UNWELCOME GUESTS

"I t's a sad thing when citizens cannot peacefully gather of an evening with friends," said Grandfather.

"I warrant it's Patrick the dragoons are after," said Joe, the tone of his voice as dark as his hair. "Let's snuff our own candles so we don't have such visitors ourselves."

But before Joe snuffed the last candle, the door burst open, and the beam of a search lantern caught the three of us. Because of the lantern's brightness, we could not see the one who held it. I threw up my hands to protect my eyes.

Joe uttered a curse, and Grandfather demanded that the lantern be put down and that those who had forced the door, leave. Bran bristled and growled the kind of growl he had growled before the attack he'd made on something or someone in the Fairy Woods. I lunged for him and held fast to his collar, for I imagined red coat soldiers with guns behind the lantern. Who else but Her Majesty's troops would enter a home without so much as a knock or hello?

Three soldiers bearing muskets stepped into the room where the remnants of the party lay all about. Our neighbors had carefully taken with them their tin cups and leftovers from the food they brought, but here and there a bottle or bit of wrapping tissue remained to show that we had entertained company.

"How dare you force your way into a citizen's cottage?" Grandfather shouted at the soldiers. His anger was strong and directed like a bullet.

"What 'citizens' would those be?" one of the dragoons said, scorn showing in the disdainful lines of his mouth. "Citizens have rights. You have none."

"Hush, corporal," said another who had an extra stripe on his sleeve. "We are not here for debate."

"Traitors we are not!" I shouted.

"Mind your tongue and that dog, girl!" the sergeant said.

He flicked his head and the other two took their lanterns and began to scout through our two rooms. Though it was easy to see that we had few hiding places, they overturned our table, and in Grandfather's bedroom, I heard them upend the bed.

"Up the ladder!" the sergeant commanded and the two climbed. I could hear them scuffling about with Joe's and my pallet beds and our pitiful collection of clothing and old schoolbooks.

"Leave off, men," Joe said, and I feared for him. "Can't you see there are only the three of us? We have done nothing, unless a birthday celebration for my sister is a danger to the Queen!"

144

The two who had gone up the ladder came down.

The dragoon sergeant pushed closer to Joe, his musket pointing to Joe's chest. "A party?" he sneered. "There may be no gathering of any kind behind four walls and a closed door. No place on this cursed island is innocent of treasonable talk. Where did your 'guests' go from here?"

"Peacefully to their own cottages where I hope they will sleep without this kind of interruption," Joe said. "I pray the three of you sleep well, if you can after such an assault as you make on this house."

Bran continued to growl and I continued to clutch him, afraid of what might happen to him and to us if he attacked one of the soldiers.

"Let's be gone," said the sergeant at last. "If these people harbored fugitives tonight, those pitiful creatures are long gone."

The dragoons left—gladly, I thought—one giving a last kick at my creepie on the way out, sending the poor thing flying. I reminded myself of what I had told Brendan on the bridge across The River Tar: These men were ignorant, bored and far from home. Now also I saw that they were dangerous and fearful. If they saw an old man, a young girl, a dog and one strong youth as enemies, what must they suspect was hiding behind each shadow and shed? How could we ever be safe with such men in our land?

⇥ CHAPTER 25 ⇤
A DIFFERENT RACE

My birthday meant an end to summer and the beginning of school. As they had the past two years, September and October signified getting ready for the Galty Prize race. By the time November rolled around, Peg was fit and ready, and, once again, I was full of hopes and anticipation.

"It's a glorious morning, Maggie, a fine day for the Galty Chase," Grandfather said, gesturing to include the hooded mountains and the fields on either side of the road.

"I see no sun, except the few rays that show from under a cap of clouds." I smiled in agreement just the same.

"Sunshine aplenty spills through your voice and shines in my heart. For all the clouds, it's still a fine, soft day for so late in the year."

We rode side by side, Grandfather on Bridey and I on Peg, whose hide I had brushed to burnished bronze. The mare's mane was a beaten sheet of copper, her tail a copper sheaf. No sun was needed to spark lights from her gleaming flanks. The two horses, one old and common, one fine and well-bred, nuzzled each other when the walk allowed.

"The course will be perfect. We've had just the right amount of rain to give a spring to the ground, not enough to turn it into a sodden trap," Grandfather said.

"Yes, it's a good day for the race," I agreed.

"Truly, Maggie, I've never seen her better. That hoof is hard as the Rock of Cashel on which Saint Patrick built his church. Her spirit is eager to run, for I see it in her eye. She's ready to run the best race seen at Galty since Boru chased the giant for a crown."

"And the trophy will be ours. Three wins, Grandfather!"

"The farm will be deeded to us, free and clear."

"Then you don't regret the bargain Joe and I made with Drummond? I'm still sorry we didn't tell you first."

"You were right to dole out the story in small pieces. I'm not sure I could have managed to swallow both the news of what winning would mean, and losing, too. Not in the same day!"

"I only regret that Joe can't be at Drummond's today. I do so want him with us. And I worry that he's in danger."

"Worry only about the race, Maggie. Joe can take care of himself. He's proud to be in the company of Patrick Connory and the patriots at Cahir. The likes of Lord and Lady Darcy will be depending on his sharp eyes to keep watch for them."

147

"But a secret meeting, Grandfather—it's one thing to stand in a square with a crowd to listen to Home Rulers speak of rights and freedom, but in secret—I don't know . . . What might happen if they are discovered?"

Grandfather shook his head and grew silent while I remembered the night of my birthday, just a few months past. I remembered the stories of imprisoned men. I remembered the redcoats with their lantern shining into every corner of our cottage and their boots scuffing our earthen floor.

Peg snorted and trotted in place, dancing on the road. Even Bridey was frisky and eager.

"A few dragoons will no doubt be among those enjoying the race at Galty, but most of the troops from Cahir Castle have once more been sent to Lismore Town," Grandfather said. "They are far away, over the Vee of the mountains. The English expect every man, woman and child in the countryside to be at Drummond's today. Cahir is the safest town in Ireland for patriots to meet."

Grandfather nudged old Bridey into a gentle trot. "Get Peg moving a little, Maggie. She needs to be breezed."

I clucked and Peg began to trot, then went to a gentle canter that sent us up the road ahead of Grandfather and Bridey. Beyond, the road inclined gently, and, surprisingly, dust rose far ahead. It would take a large troop to raise dust on the road after the light rains of the previous days.

I pulled Peg up and waited, puzzled at first. But long before Grandfather reached me, my eyes had read the message.

"What is it, girl?" Grandfather said, but the tremor in his voice told me that he, too, saw the dust and was thinking, *Soldiers!* He also would be thinking, *Trap!*

"They're heading back to Cahir, Grandfather. Someone has informed!"

"Joe's in danger!" Grandfather whispered, and it was the same thought that was squeezing my own brain. Joe, Patrick and Lady Darcy! Finnegan and the others!

I began to turn Peg, my hands knowing what my mind had not yet understood.

"I've got to warn them, Grandfather," I told him softly, reaching a hand to brush my grandfather's cheek, as though he had shed tears that needed wiping.

"The race, Maggie. Think what it means!" He placed a restraining hand on the mare's bridle.

"It means everything, Grandfather." I touched his hand. "But nothing without Joe." The words stood between us. I saw the misery in his eyes, as he took his hand from Peg's bridle.

"You must ride fast. And be wary, Maggie, for this will not be the only troop. Others may come from the east or south."

I reached across the space between the horses and touched Grandfather's hand, leaning to kiss his cheek.

"God ride with you, Maggie," he said, his voice full of sadness and pride.

"And with you," I said, my heart full of the moment.

I set Peg down the road at a gallop, racing to put as much distance as possible between myself and the dragoons. I must not be stopped. The need was too urgent. Peg responded with her great heart.

When I could no longer see the cloud of dust over my shoulder, I slowed Peg to conserve her for the long ride ahead. Hours would pass before we reached Cahir, hours during which riders would gather at Drummond's. The flag would come down and the race would be run. Joe and I had flung our dreams and future like a wager of coins rung down on a counter, the outcome of the race determining our fate. Now, for us, for Peg and me, a different race was building. If this new race was lost, so might be lives. Penalties were levied against those assembling in secret. My brother and our friends must not be caught.

But the other race still remained, and, while another horse and rider gathered glory, Drummond would gather all I held dear. I must not think of that now. All Peg's and my energy and concentration must go toward getting to Cahir in time.

And time was a great unknown. I could easily outpace the dragoons marching and riding behind me, but Grandfather had warned that soldiers would be coming from other directions. How far were those soldiers from the town? When would they arrive in Cahir?

Last year's ride to Cahir stood in my mind, and I wished for Brendan riding next to me now. How much braver I would feel with his resolve and quick mind beside my doubts and tumbling thoughts. We had sung then of Irish heroes and martyrs. By night, others might be martyred, perhaps before noon.

Ahead in Cahir, Joe and Patrick plotted with Lady Darcy, her husband and the others. They would be choosing words and strategies, perhaps drinking tea or porter and eating bread and stew. Around them, marching and riding, dragoons would close in from several directions. I imagined rough hands on Lady Darcy's slender arms. I saw boots and guns, ropes binding my brother's wrists and looped around his neck for a halter. I heard guns and imagined Patrick's body splashed with blood.

My spinning brain nearly became my undoing. I rounded a bend in the road and found myself trotting head on into a pair of mounted dragoons, young men with faces nearly as red as their coats.

"Hold up!" shouted one of the men, seizing Peg's bridle near the bit. I looked across the necks of the horses into a round face bearded by a few scraps of hair the color of straw. "You've put a head of steam on that horse. To what purpose, lass?"

I was terrified. Peg snorted and backed away from the restraining hands of the soldier.

"Please, mister," I said, amazed at how readily a lie formed on my lips. "My aunt is ill—only a way down the road. I'm just on my way to her cottage and thought I'd have a gallop."

"That's a fine horse, and with your boots and fine clothes, you don't look like the ordinary peasant hereabouts. What's your name?" The dragoon's voice was nasal and harsh. He looked no older than Brendan, but his eyes were wary and dangerous.

"Answer, girl," the other soldier said. He was slightly older, I saw, and squinted at me from the face of a fish. "Your name, girl!"

"Maggie, sir. We're from the north, my family. Come down for the races at Drummond's. We got word about my aunt, who, as I said, lives nearby, and I was sent . . ."

"It wouldn't be that your aunt is in Cahir plotting treason?" snarled the round-faced soldier.

151

But the other soldier dragged at Peg's bridle to turn her around. He slapped the mare on the rump. "Be gone," he said, and I had no choice but to obey.

I galloped Peg back toward Drummond's, but only until we were out of sight around the bend.

"Peg, you've got to take this hedgerow as you've taken no other."

Pegasus flew the hedgerow and raced cross-country away from the road. Effortlessly, she took wall after wall. For this she'd trained all her life.

Fearing greatly for my brother, but nevertheless exhilarated, I moved with Peg. I crouched high on her neck to take a pasture wall, rising in the saddle to the rhythm of the trot, or leaning to guide her across the fields. I concentrated on the ride and put the menace of soldiers and guns from my mind. Time paced us, but time would not overtake us any more than had any of the fine steeplechasers at Galty in years past. We should be in Cahir before noon.

"You'll do it, Peg. You'll take me in plenty of time to warn Joe and the others."

She responded with ears pricked forward. She needed no urging and little guidance. *I am the wind itself*, her flying body said.

At midday, we reached the last pasture wall before the foothills, and I rested Peg beside a stream that I knew would eventually cross the road again on its way to the River Suir. I allowed the mare a few slurps from the flowing water and a few blades of grass before we went on, following the stream.

We rode along the banks, a path beaten by years of men and women fishing. When the banks became too brushy or the road came too near and I feared we might be seen, I took Peg to the shallow stream itself.

Finally, with nothing further to conceal us, we had gone as far as we could without rejoining the road. We emerged from the protective trees and gorse to find the way clear in both directions. I now had a straight gallop to Cahir. I prayed that the dragoons were far behind.

Rested from the slow pace of the river and the riverbanks, Peg put herself full out on the road, her hooves clattering over the bridge to Cahir. I scarcely noted the emptiness of the town or the quiet of the castle as we galloped by.

I pulled Peg to a skidding stop in front of the Cahir House Hotel, knowing I should start my search there. I tossed Peg's reins to a young man wearing a green scarf about his neck.

"You can't pass . . . " the young man began, but he must have seen desperation written on my face, for he stepped to take Peg's bridle. "I'll hide her for you. Go on inside."

Once inside the door to the curtained public room, I leaned against it and looked for a familiar face.

A man, his short, round bulk silhouetted by light from a window, rose as I entered. Even in the poor light, I recognized the wild hair and shape of Finnegan, the poet.

"It's Shannon's sister; is it not?" he asked in his rich western voice. He held a glass of porter in his large hand as he came round the table toward me.

I began to blurt out my tale, but Finnegan hushed me and steered me out the back door of the room and onto stairs that led to a large dark cellar.

He led me through a passage that took us beneath the street to another cellar beneath a different house. "It's the curse of Ireland that we must be always watching for spies," he muttered. "You have something dire to tell us, I know, but you can say it to all once you're with the others." A lounging lad with a candle let us pass into a small, damp room.

Five men were gathered around a small table, Patrick and a man I took to be Lord Darcy among them. Lady Darcy was there. All stood at my hurried entrance with Finnegan. They must have known by my face what I had to tell them, for they asked no questions, but only waited for me to say it.

"There's little time," I finished. "You must hide yourselves."

Patrick said, "They'll take Cahir apart stone by stone to search us out."

"We must flee," said Finnegan and began to gather papers and stuff them into saddlebags.

I followed him from the small room and met my brother on the stairs.

"Maggie!" Joe said, taking my arm to lead me farther up the stairs. "The race? What's happened?"

"There's no race for Peg this year, Joe. The dragoons are on their way to find this place. I rode to warn you."

Joe looked stricken. The fate of Shannon Farm rose between us like a ghost, but he hugged me to him and said, "You did a brave thing. Now you must go home with care." His voice was clotted. "Take no more risks."

My brother's arms around me filled me with love, and relief that I had found him in time. "Come home with me," I said. "You can ride behind. Peg can carry us both."

He pulled away from me. "Maggie," he said, "you must do nothing to draw attention to yourself. It's bad enough you have that showy horse without adding suspicions by carrying a rider. Don't worry. I'm not important enough to be known. I'll make my way home safely."

Before I could object, the others were with us.

Patrick said, "Horses are waiting in front. Those of us who might be recognized must go quickly. Take to the fields and try not to be seen. The rest of you must act as if you are doing no more than marketing or visiting. We'll need luck and the blessing of God to escape, but without warning . . . " He nodded toward me. "We'd be spending the night in the castle dungeons for sure."

Outside, horses stood saddled and ready for the patriots. Lord and Lady Darcy had pulled rough cloaks over their fine clothes and mounted quickly. From her sorrel mare, Lady Darcy reached for my hand.

I felt a smooth, warm object against my palm and Lady Darcy closed my fist around it. "You have my ring," the lady said. "With it my servants will give you entrance to my house at any time. Please bring it to me if ever you need my help. We'll be ever grateful for what you've done today. It seems I now owe you two great favors."

I began to reply, but Lady Darcy had wheeled her horse and galloped hard on the heels of her husband, heading north. Finnegan rode south and others east, west and points in between. Patrick walked his horse beside Joe and me as we went back to Cahir House to collect Peg.

"You weren't seen?" Patrick asked.

"Only once. Soldiers stopped me, but afterwards, I went cross-country."

"You must be careful not to be recognized. Take a basket as I told the others and pretend you are here on errands. You should be safe enough; the soldiers will have their sights on catching bigger fry than you." But his looks betrayed that he feared for me, too.

I searched Patrick's face. He was only twenty-two, but I saw lines in his face, and a raw scar broke dangerously through the eyebrow and onto his cheek. It hadn't been there the night of my birthday party.

Patrick embraced me, and I ached to think that today might see him shot or thrust into prison.

The young man mounted, whipped his horse to a gallop, and was quickly gone.

"Joe, how can it be right?" I searched my brother's face through a teary mist. "Can't men and women meet in peace to plan for a better future? Is it wrong to want to be free of laws given by strangers?"

As I stood at Peg's head, Joe pressed a basket of onions into my hand. I opened my hand to take the basket and something fell and rang on the stones at my feet. The ring! I retrieved Lady Darcy's gift and pushed it reverently onto my own finger.

The ring was simple, but engraved on it was a crest, a Celtic knot, a symbol of eternity.

Joe urged me to mount, and I pulled myself onto Peg's saddle. I leaned to kiss my brother and turned the mare toward the bridge, the basket clenched tightly between Peg's neck and the reins.

With my other hand, I twisted the ring on my finger to hide the Darcy crest, and thought of a woman with lands and wealth, and me, a girl with no possessions— now not even the wonderful horse on which I rode. Lady Darcy had shared her passion for freedom with me. I'd lost Peg to Drummond, but the ring promised I'd never stand alone.

⊰ CHAPTER 26 ⊱

BULLETS AND TREASON

I clutched the basket of onions along with Pegasus' reins. The basket might be filled with the treasure of Ireland and the reins, a lifeline I dare not drop. When I saw the gray stones of the castle and the broad bridge, I felt my heartbeat in my hands as well as in my chest.

I prayed I'd be able to cross the bridge before any soldiers returned. So far, just the one guard still stood at the castle gate. But by the time I reached the center of the bridge, with its views—either side of the wide, peaceful river and straight ahead to the road leading from town—a troop of red-coated dragoons began to cross, heading toward me.

I resisted the urge to turn and set Pegasus running in the opposite direction, back toward town. Instead, I tried to think of myself as a farm girl going home from market, no more on my mind than to reach my hearth and stretch my feet to the fire. I forced myself to look away from the soldiers as they marched by, but I glimpsed wicked muskets held at the ready, and the thought of those guns prickled my skin with fear.

I waited until I was far down the road and around a bend from the soldiers before I risked a trot. I hadn't trotted far when I heard other hooves pounding behind me. An English voice shouted, "The woman said the poet took this road at a run."

Looking for Finnegan, the mounted soldiers galloped by. I might have been a rock in a current of water except that the eyes of one touched mine as he passed. The fish-faced dragoon who had stopped me that morning on the way to Cahir.

He knew me. But he didn't stop. When he had time, he'd remember. He'd know I'd lied and disobeyed.

Dry trees cracked in the wind. I flinched away from the sound, but no trees were falling. No wind bit my cheeks. It must have been musket fire, not breaking branches, that I heard. My throat burned. I prayed silently and fervently for Joe. For Patrick. For Lady Darcy. For Finnegan.

I kept to the road that would lead me away from Cahir and toward home. With each breath, I expected to hear more shots or see the dragoons returning. Had they found Finnegan? Would they take me, too? I saw no one for a long while. When I did, I had time to lead Peg through a broken gate into an empty yard. I hid the mare and myself behind the ruined walls of an old cottage and allowed myself to relax.

"Enjoy a bit of grazing, girl. You deserve it." Before she bent her head to graze, Peg nuzzled my arm.

While we hid, shadows lengthened around us. When we were able to return safely to the road, afternoon was turning toward evening.

Something rustled in the tall grass beside the road, and Peg shied and turned toward the noise, her ears laid back. She snorted as a head of wild, black hair popped from a grass-grown ditch. It was Finnegan, and I called his name in surprise.

"Hush, girl. You'll give me away," the poet said.

I rode to the ditch, and Peg stretched her neck to nudge the man. "It's all right," I said. "I haven't seen any soldiers for a while."

The poet crawled out from his hiding place, wearing weeds and leaves in his hair and on his coat. A green scarf circled the throat that had sung the beautiful Irish words in front of Cahir House not many months before. He smiled broadly, and I could see that the danger swirling around us excited him.

"The dragoons were gaining on me," he said. "So I let my horse do the running without me. They'll soon be back on my trail, but perhaps dark will come before then. They have no bloodhounds that I've seen."

A lone rider pounded toward us, and Finnegan dived back to the ditch. I looked frantically for somewhere to hide Peg. High fences stood along each side of the road and beyond them I saw no cover.

Peg pranced and whinnied at the approaching horse and rider. The horse became a strong black shape. Cashel! The rider called my name.

Brendan slid Cashel to a stop, dismounting while the dust swirled around the horse's hooves. He was still dressed for the race at Drummond's.

I, too, dismounted and folded myself into his arms. Since the night of my party, I had been unable to see or think of Brendan without the memory of his lips hard on mine, now he was holding me again.

The poet once more climbed out from the ditch.

"Oh, Brendan, I'm so afraid," I said. "The dragoons are in Cahir. I can only hope Joe and Patrick have got away. You see Mr. Finnegan here. He's the only one I know about for sure."

Brendan hugged me, and I felt encouraged by the strength of his arms and his breath against my cheek.

"I've been afraid, too," he said. "Afraid for Patrick and the others. Afraid for you, Maggie. Especially for you, Maggie. I came from Drummond's as soon as I spoke with your grandfather and found what you'd done." He released me and turned to Finnegan.

"Was the warning in time? Do you think the others got away?"

"I know only my own case," Finnegan answered. "I've had them hot on my heels, but I'm still here to tell the tale. With verses to build around the bravery of this young girl."

"Maggie," Brendan said. "Did any English see you in Cahir?"

I told him about the two soldiers who had stopped me and how I rode cross-country to avoid them. I told him about seeing one of the soldiers again later.

"Then we'd better go cross-country to home now. We mustn't take a chance. They'll know you for the one who warned the men at the meeting."

He turned to the poet. "Mr. Finnegan, you should take Cashel. I'll get up behind Maggie. You can't hide in a ditch the rest of your life."

"No thanks, lad," the poet said. "I'm glad enough to be out of the saddle, for I'm more comfortable with my feet on God's green earth. I know a house not far from here, with a warm bed and bottles of stout to welcome me. I'll wait for night and make my way there. Wish me luck and be on your way."

Brendan and I were not far from where we left Finnegan when three dragoons galloped up behind us. They skidded their horses to a stop, blocking escape from either direction, and began to question Brendan.

"Have you seen a man with dark hair in a great hurry to be gone? He was wearing a tweed coat and had a green scarf at his neck."

"Many would fit that description."

"This was the poet, Finnegan. You'd better answer straight, lad." The dragoon squinted his eyes at Brendan and menaced him with a scowl. "It's treason not to help Her Majesty's troops do their duty." Treason meant the gallows or a shot in the back of the neck.

I gripped Peg's reins until the blood left my knuckles. Sweat gathered in my palms. Chills began again at my back.

"I didn't see him," Brendan answered.

"And you, lass, what about you?"

I shook my head and studied my clenched hands and the basket of onions.

"My sister knows nothing," Brendan said. "We are just on our way home from market."

"It takes two Irishmen to buy onions!" laughed one of the British.

My anger rose hotly at the joke.

The mood of the soldiers again menaced. The one with stripes on his sleeve put his hand on Cashel's bridle. "How do you come by these horses?" he demanded. "Donkeys are for Irishmen to ride."

"We're going to Drummond House. There's a race," I blurted.

"What race? You're late for that!" one soldier sneered.

"More like revolution, I'll wager," said the leader. "Come with us. We'll let them decide at the castle whether you'll go on."

A soldier reached for Peg's bridle when two more of his fellows galloped up. The fish-faced horseman!

For a moment the dragoons who had been questioning us turned to greet their comrades.

Brendan leaned toward me. "Take Peg over the fields. Meet me later at the Fairy Woods."

I tossed the onion basket aside and searched the road for a place to get through or over the fence.

Behind me, a dragoon yelled, "Stop that girl! She's a traitor!"

Over my shoulder, I saw Brendan kick Cashel through the midst of the soldiers. "Go, Maggie," he called to me.

In the confusion of squealing horses, the leader of the soldiers remained steady. He raised his musket to his shoulder and aimed at Brendan's fleeing back.

I wheeled Peg and charged the man and his horse. The musket went off with a roar, but harmlessly at the sky. At a gallop, Peg and I left a tangle of soldiers trying to control their mounts, grouping themselves for pursuit. Over my shoulder, I saw two gallop after Brendan, but he was already far down the road. They'd never catch up to Cashel. The one I had charged was off his horse and reloading. Two others spurred their horses after me.

I led my pursuers straight down the road away from Brendan. Instead of fences, now tall hedgerows lined one side of the road, and an even taller stone wall guarded the other. Ahead, the road curved. I put Peg at the wall as if it were a hurdle on the Galty course. I leaned well up on Peg's neck, gripped the copper mane with my hands and Peg's sides with my legs. Peg sailed over the wall, her rear hooves ticking the stones at the top.

Behind me, I heard calls of confusion. The soldiers would be readying their horses to have a go at the same wall Peg had cleared. Angry shouts from the men, squeals from the horses told me that the horses had refused. Let them try again if they dared. My blood ran hot with excitement. They'd never catch Peg now. The mare was in a full-out run across an open field, headed for the trout stream and the foothills. The soldiers had given up the chase. Though I heard the bark of guns, no bullets found me as I fled.

Once into the trees that clumped around the stream that led to the Fairy Woods, I brought Peg to a stop. While we rested, I looked in all directions. Nothing. What should I do?

Somewhere on the road and across the countryside British soldiers searched for me. They had shot at me! I squeezed my eyes shut. Would I wake safe at home, ready to set out for Drummond's and the Galty Race? I opened my eyes. Surely, my life couldn't have led me to this place where I had ridden Peg into the dangers of bullets and treason.

But, of course, it wasn't a dream. The long ride to Cahir, the poet taking me through secret halls to a small room. Patrick, Joe, and the Darcys—the whole of the day was vivid to me, and I knew I was wide-awake.

"Oh, Peg," I said, "where is Brendan?"

He should be riding this way by now. Why hadn't I seen him? I closed my eyes and remembered the sound of the guns. What if the soldiers hadn't been firing at me at all. What if . . . ? Not Brendan, I prayed. Not Patrick or Joe.

163

Slowly, I turned Peg to walk beside the stream back toward home. Brendan had told me to meet him at the Fairy Woods. He would be there. Perhaps the others, too.

But when I reached the fringes of the woods, the emptiness of the little grove announced itself with a quiet that was absolute. No branches stirred in the wind. Not even an insect or bird voice broke the stillness. How could I have ever felt this place was full of magic and fairy beings? It was haunted now only by emptiness, and emptiness haunted me as well.

Breaking the quiet, Peg snorted and entered the woods, ruffling the brown leaves with her hooves and sending up the steam of her sweat into the air. Peg carried me to the edge of the clearing where I had built the leprechaun trap three years before.

I dismounted, briefly hugged Peg's strong neck, then led the tired horse through the clearing and past the Druid altars and cairns. I had never realized what a small place the woods were, no room for friends to miss each other. No room to hide from an enemy if one should come looking. Fear filled my heart and stabbed my stomach. Fear for myself, fear for Brendan.

The dark woods became darker as day faded, and I pulled my shawl tighter around my shoulders.

"Oh, Peg," I sighed. "Somewhere they were running horse races and winning prizes today. Have we won not even the safety of our friends?" I loosened Peg's saddle and let the mare graze the verge of the woods.

Settling wearily to the ground, my back to a tree, for moments I lost myself in visions of the day, trying to call the loved faces to my mind, but I found I was unable to quite draw in the lines that defined Joe, couldn't quite bring the colors of hair or eyes to Brendan or Patrick. I remembered the comfort of Brendan's arms and wished for him here. But closed eyes didn't close out the remembered sounds of shots and English voices. Then something else—crashing, not shots this time, but the cracking and breaking of real branches. A horse was pounding through the woods.

I stood, panic flooding my veins. Should I run? Should I hope? Peg whinnied, and a horse whinnied back. Then hooves, their sound muffled by the soft forest floor, approached slowly.

I heard my name called and answered, "Brendan. Brendan, I'm here."

Tears of overwhelming relief flooded my eyes. Everything would be all right with Brendan here at last. I reached him as he slid from Cashel's back to take me in his arms. He held me close, and I felt the strong pounding of his heart.

I wrapped my arms around him and felt him relax against me. His arms loosened, and I realized that I was keeping him from collapse.

Then his full weight was against me, and it took all my strength to prevent him from falling, except gently, to the ground. I cradled his unconscious head and saw the line of torn sleeve and caked blood at his shoulder. In the dimming light of evening, my heart pounding, I tore the shredded sleeve from Brendan's upper arm. The wound was an ugly gash, but I was relieved to see no fresh blood. I touched below and above the wound and felt heat and puffiness, but no bullet. The flesh had been ripped, but the bullet must have passed on by.

He moved and groaned.

"Oh, Brendan. You've been shot," I said.

He groaned again and lifted himself onto his elbow. "It's little, Maggie . . . a scratch." He shook his head wearily and looked into my eyes. "The poet is dead. And, but for you spoiling the soldier's aim, I would be too."

Brendan pulled himself farther, to a sitting position leaning against the tree, one knee bent. I knelt beside him to watch his face for pain, but I saw only exhaustion.

"Finnegan . . . "

I blocked his words with my hand. "No. Tell me later. You need rest."

But he had to go on, it seemed, for when I took my hand from his mouth he began again. "More soldiers . . . where we left Finnegan. The poet jumped onto the road . . . took a musket blast meant for me." He closed his eyes, and I let him lean back against the tree. "After that I put Cashel over some walls. Except for the wound, I got away clean."

I used Peg's saddle blanket to make Brendan more comfortable, and he slept. I found a water bottle tied to Cashel's saddle and used the water to wet my friend's forehead and dampen his lips. I mixed some of the water with dirt from the forest floor and pressed the mud to Brendan's arm. It might prove as healing as mud from the River Tar had been for Pegasus's hoof so long ago.

Then, through the long, dark hours, I watched, glad for Brendan's even breathing and the presence of the horses—their occasional snorts and movements as they shifted their weight in sleep.

In the morning I would have to find a way to get Brendan to the cottage and let his mother know that he was safe. At the cottage, I would learn the fate of Joe and my friends. Later would come other confrontations. Drummond would claim Peg and the farm. He would hand us passage and let us gather our poor belongings.

What would become of Grandfather? He had collapsed after the second Galty running, and though he was stronger than ever now, what might happen when he saw his cottage roof torn down and its shed put to the torch so that no vagabonds would shelter there?

He had learned to hope again. Could the new strength carry him forward to better days in America? A picture bloomed in my mind. Joe and Grandfather stood before a small house surrounded by green fields in a place with an Indian name, a place I had never seen on a map. I closed my eyes tightly and tried to set myself into that picture, but other shapes crowded me out. I hugged my legs and rested my cheek on my knees and tried to look into the future. Where was Brendan in that future?

When I opened my eyes again, the dark, moonless night was giving way to dawn. By earliest glimmer in the east, I started to wake Brendan. I felt stiff and cold from the night spent outdoors.

"Can you make it to the cottage?" I asked. "We'll be safe there for a while. The British can't know yet who we are. Can you get onto Cashel if I help?" Gently, I sponged his forehead.

He didn't respond, and I feared he was deep in fever. But I repeated my questions several times, until he lifted himself onto his elbow and let me help him.

He stood with great difficulty, leaning weakly against me, but managed to pull himself onto Cashel's saddle. He kept himself there with me walking at the horse's side to give encouragement. Pegasus walked behind.

We made our way beside the woods to the road and then, seeing the road clear, continued on to Shannon cottage, a lonely path with an uncertain scene at the end.

◄ CHAPTER 27 ►

NEW BEGINNINGS

Later, with Brendan's wound salved and bandaged, we tucked him into Grandfather's cot. With the horses fed, watered and hidden in the barn, I sat with Joe and Grandfather. Each of us had a bowl of cabbage soup and a slab of soda bread in place upon the table.

"If they find him here and wounded, they'll take him away, no questions asked," Joe said of Brendan. "And like as not, pull down the cottage, too."

"And Maggie?" asked Grandfather. "Do you think they'll be after her?"

"You said yourself, Grandfather, that the race meeting buzzed with rumors about the English trap. And you said that she was missed."

"Drummond was in a stew. He thought that Maggie had taken Pegasus and run off rather than chance losing her."

"What did you tell him?" I asked.

"I said you'd had a spill the day before, nothing serious, but Peg is limping and couldn't run."

"Did he believe you?"

"Doubtless not. It's his habit to disbelieve whatever we say. In this case, he'll rightly figure that it was you who rode to Cahir, as soon as someone mentions to him that it was a red-haired girl on a chestnut horse."

"Then what can we do?"

"We must buy some time," Joe said. "I'll go to Drummond. I'll make it clear to Sir Henry that if he has any suspicions of Maggie, he must keep them to himself or never see Pegasus in his pastures. He can bloody well swallow his duty, for I'd no way deliver him a sound horse at the price of my sister. He must see us safely off to America, as he promised."

"Someone will tell."

"Eventually. It's a bit of time only. But, if we make it through today, by dark I'll take you and Brendan to Mitchelstown in Bridey's cart. Chances are Patrick is already there, sheltering in the caves."

"We can all meet again in Kinsale," Grandfather said. "Drummond can start our passages to the New World with fare on a fishing boat to Liverpool."

"Kinsale to Liverpool and then on to Boston," I mused, trying out the sounds. "Kinsale, Liverpool, Boston," I said again, but the words wouldn't fill up with meaning.

"And then to the farmlands," said Joe. "Farms are big as counties. States called Iowa and Illinois are vast as Ireland. We'll find a place in America. You'll never worry again about debts and foreclosures, I promise."

"How can you be sure?" I asked.

169

"It's a country of laws for even the lowest, Maggie. We can work for our dreams and be sure that work will count."

"Do you believe that, too, Grandfather?"

For answer, Grandfather turned to Joe and jogged his arm. "Tell her the rest, Joe. Tell her the rest of it." He spoke eagerly, and my heart lifted to the note of hope in his voice. What Pegasus had rekindled in Grandfather hadn't died with the dream of winning the race.

Joe reached across the table for my hand. A closeness had grown between us since sealing the bargain with Drummond. Yesterday, when we had stood on that stairway in Cahir with all our dreams dissolving, I had felt the touch of his love as well as heard his words of caution and fear for my safety. Now again, I felt that same love from my brother as he shared his new dream.

"Some of this is still to be settled," he said to me, "but Grandfather and I are sure that we can get money from the sale of our animals, money that will help us with a start in America. Bridey, of course, we won't sell. Mr. Connory will take her and care for her for the few good years of work left in her. But the cows, the chickens and pigs . . . given time, Mr. Connory can sell them and send the coin to us in America." He paused, then added, "And Mrs. Connory has promised to make a place at her hearth for Bran."

I smiled at his enthusiasm.

Joe leaned closer to me. "But that isn't the best, Maggie," he said. "Nan Connory knows of the bargain with Drummond. She agreed to marry me whether or not we won and kept the farm or we emigrated." The expression on his face was one of joy—an expression I had seldom seen there.

I leaped up and came around the table and Joe rose to meet me. "Oh, Joe, I'm glad," I said over and over while my tears of happiness fell on his shoulder. "I'm so glad."

Yesterday, I had not been able to form a picture from the words, Kinsale . . . Liverpool . . . Boston. The vision I'd had of the cottage in America with Grandfather and Joe swam forward once more into my brain. I had not belonged in that picture. Now, Nan Connory stood inside the frame. Beside my brother and grandfather.

"I will have a sister," I said, kissing Joe. "To keep company with you and Grandfather in my heart." It was as close as I could come for now to tell them that I would not be going with them. I had only just come to know that for myself.

Joe left on Bridey to see Drummond to "buy the time" that he felt he needed for Brendan and me. He would also make arrangements at the mill to leave our animals with Brendan's father. He would tell Brendan's mother that Brendan had been slightly wounded, but that he'd mend.

Grandfather went to the shed to see to the cows, and I brought my old three-legged creepie into the bedroom to sit beside Brendan.

"Joe has gone to the mill. He'll likely bring your mother and Nan to you," I said as Brendan fluttered his eyelids and began to wake. "Later, by dark, he'll take you to Mitchelstown. No doubt your brother is there already."

"You should come to Mitchelstown, too, Maggie. You'll need to hide for awhile. There's no mistaking your flaming hair and your beautiful horse. Someone will put two and two together before long."

171

"It's what Joe fears, too. But Lady Darcy has offered me her help. I want to go to Dublin instead."

"Lady Darcy? Yes, that's good. That's better. You'll be comfortable with her. You can come back before long. The English will forget about you as other foxes come along for them to hound."

"I won't come back, Brendan."

He lifted himself onto his elbow and faced me squarely. "Of course you will. You'll come home!"

"And where will my home be?" I said, asking the question of the air more than of my friend. Then, meeting his look, I told him of the bargain with Drummond and finished, "The farm will go to Sir Henry. And Peg, too."

"He can't hold you to that!"

I smiled. There was no need to answer Brendan, for he would realize without being told that Drummond could do as he liked.

"In return we are to emigrate. Drummond will give passage to the three of us to America."

"All your dreams of the race, your dreams for your family . . . " Brendan mourned. "It's too hard."

"The dreams are unreal to me now. Do you remember how I paid for Peg with a fairy gift? Grandfather said the gift might be turned against me."

"Is that what you think?"

"Not now. Fairy magic is nothing compared to the wickedness done by greedy landlords and English law. Here we always pay beyond the price for what we get. Finnegan with his blood for a bit of poetry. Joe and me with broken hearts for wanting land and safety for ourselves and Grandfather."

Brendan sat stunned, while I went on, "I haven't told Grandfather and Joe yet, but I'm not going with them. At first, I thought I must go, too, but now I'm sure they'll be all right without me. They are reconciled to going—maybe even eager. Grandfather hopes to find his lost sisters, and . . . Brendan, you should know . . . Your sister is going with Joe."

It was another blow for Brendan to absorb, and he grew pale. "I knew Joe had spoken to her. But I didn't know about America. My mother will grieve."

"She'll have you and Patrick. Just as Grandfather will have Nan and Joe," I said, and we sat in silence for awhile.

"But what about you, Maggie? Will you come to the mill with me? My mother loves you. And someday . . . "

"No, Brendan," I interrupted. "I'll not stay in Tipperary. I love all of you, too . . . " Here I placed my hand on Brendan's. "I want to go further in school. Your mother suggested it to me, and Lady Darcy will help me. I'll be a teacher, maybe. You said yourself that Ireland had need of me. I've thought of Finnegan. Did his words mean nothing? Did his death mean nothing?"

"How can I let you go? I would go with you if I could, but I'm needed at home. Patrick has already given himself to the cause of freedom, and now Nan will be going away."

Brendan's face had grown pale as the pillows he leaned against, and I feared for him.

Outside, the sun was fighting with another cloudy day and winning. Dapples of light spilled over the bedclothes and brightened Brendan's pale eyes. He was feeling the same pain that had stabbed me last night in the woods, and I squeezed his hand to let him know I understood.

"We won't lose each other," I promised. "I can't see myself live out my days without being with you again."

173

"Then don't go," he said. With effort, he swung himself to sit on the edge of the bed, dislodging my hand that had been pressed over his, then grabbing the lost fingers. The color had returned to his cheeks.

"I must have a new life," I said. "I want to help put back the history and language the English have taken."

"The English will leave."

"I want to see that day. I want to help make that day happen."

"It's what Patrick says."

"Someone must right the wrongs."

He released my fingers, but continued to sit on the edge of the bed, the look in his eyes trying to hold me. "It's a great slice you're carving for your life," he said.

"It'll take a great slice to make up for the pieces that are being taken. My family, my home, and Peg . . . you. But somehow I know that Grandfather and Joe and Nan will prosper."

"And the mare?"

"Don't worry about Peg. She'll be well off at Drummond House, eating English oats and sending Irish colts to win English races. You'll visit her for me and tell me how she does." I shook away the pain of saying those words.

Brendan pushed off the bedding and knelt beside me. He put his hands on my shoulders, and I leaned forward till my head rested against his chest.

"Someday," he promised me.

"Someday," I promised back.

After I left Brendan, tucked back in Grandfather's bed, I found Pegasus pulling at the grass around the fence posts of the paddock.

"Come, Peg," I called. "I've brought you a carrot."

174

Peg moved across the paddock, her golden-brown eyes alive with eagerness, more for the touch of my hands than for the carrot.

"You ran a fine race to Cahir, girl," I told her. "Together we saved lives. The life we lost proved that."

I spared a moment for Finnegan, praying for his memory, his words, and his rest. He had been a fine man, full of poetry and fire.

Pegasus took the carrot now and munched it placidly.

I placed a hand high on Peg's withers and an arm around her neck, leaning hard against the warm, silky shoulder.

"Oh, Peg," I whispered. "It wasn't to end this way. Dreams and wishes die hard. But dead they are, and it's time for hopes and plans to take their place. You never belonged to me, not even a leprechaun's penny could truly buy you. We belong to each other and always will. Sir Henry Drummond can halter you and lead you away, but we will always be racing together in our hearts."

Peg pushed against my chest, her eyes pools of knowing. *Yes, I know. I understand. Always I will be looking for you. And always, you will be coming to ride.*

Tears still wet on my face from saying goodbye to Peg, I hugged Joe and then Grandfather. When I told them I would not be going with them, they forbade me to stay behind; then, knowing the iron in my will, they pleaded, until we said our tearful goodbyes and made our promises. It must not be the last time for us to meet. I'd come to them sometime in America to visit. They would return home.

I took the coins Joe offered and the bread and potatoes that Grandfather had tied up for me. I wore Brendan's oversized coat and put my red hair under his cap to disguise myself. With a pack of clothing slung over my shoulder, I mounted old Bridey and started down the road to Cahir where I would take the train to Dublin. From there, I would find a way to reach the Darcy's. Bridey would be left at a friend's house until Joe could collect her.

I had set out to bring back hope to Grandfather's life. And I had done that with Peg's help. Now it was time for Dublin. My heart raced ahead. I began to remember how winning felt.

GLOSSARY

Big House	where the British Landowner lived and collected rents from his tenants
bullock	neutered male calf, a steer
cockrow	dawn
creepie	small three-legged stool
cudgel	short heavy stick, a club
dragoon	British soldier, a "red coat" mounted or on foot
Druids	legendary race of small men inhabiting Ireland in ancient times
Fenians	an Irish group pursuing the overthrow of British rule
guinea	gold British coin, worth a little more than one English pound, less than two American dollars today, a lot of money to Maggie's family
hedgerow	bushes planted to form a fence
home rule	the desire of Irish men and women to govern themselves
lazy bed	hillside planted in potatoes, in which the seed potato is knifed into the soil
Magistrate	the dispenser of English law
mattock	tool used to pry rocks from the soil
pallet bed	mattress stuffed with hay
poteen or pocheen	Irish whiskey
rack rent	rent that placed an unfair burden on a tenant
shed	barn
steeplechase	cross-country horse race
stirabout	porridge, oatmeal
tinker	Gypsy, primarily one who mended tin pots
the Union	Ireland was considered a part of Great Britain and laws for Ireland were made in the English Parliament without Irish representation

Printed in the United States
R1903700002B/R19037PG40732LVSX00002B/1-102